Alex, Cherokee Assassin

Book One

I0531584

James A. McGregor

Southern Sunsets Publications

Alex, Cherokee Assassin

Book One

Cover Design & Interior Layout by Sarai Weaver

ISBN: 978-0-9984398-1-5

Southern Sunsets Publications

Georgetown, Florida

ACKNOWLEDGEMENTS

I could not have finished this book without the help and inspiration of a number of people. I thank Sarai Weaver for her attention to detail and style plus her editorial skills and insights about the writer's world; my daughter, Megan, for her ongoing help, patience and guidance with my writing skills; my friends, business associates and dozens of acquaintances whose personalities helped create the personas of the book's characters; and to my wife, Christel, for her endless patience and support.

Dedication:

This book is dedicated to the millions of the Native Americans who have for centuries been mistreated and maligned by the leaders of the United States Government, States Governments, and millions of our country's citizens.

Alex, Cherokee Assassin

Book One

By James A. McGregor

Introduction

"Warriors remain an integral part of each society, civilized and uncivilized. A primary role of one group of warriors is assassination for revenge on behalf of his or her society."

How do warriors evolve into being specialists in revenge killing and assassinations? How does a highly intelligent, attractive, athletic 32-year old college graduate and fitness instructor become a 21st century assassin or murder-for-hire warrior? This is a story of one such person and one of the many adventures of assassin Alex Cowart.

Chapter One

The Hunt Begins

New Orleans is one of the world's most fascinating cities – It's home to a truly unique melting pot of culture, food and music. The Mississippi River accommodates paddlewheel boats and shipping freighters from around the globe. It is truly one of Americas most culturally and historically rich destinations. For Alex Cowart, New Orleans is a destination for an assassination. The magnificent aspects of the city are a significant distraction to her mission. The details of her mission bring a unique view of the City and an assassination in such a unique and dynamic setting.

Alexandria Hope Cowart, Age 32, lives in Jacksonville, Florida. Alex is a single, straight, self-employed fitness instructor who lives a second life as an assassin performing special missions for revenge killing.

August 11, 2015, 3:55 pm

Alex arrived at her hotel for the night, the Marriott Hotel on Canal Street, New Orleans, Louisiana; and parked on the third floor of the parking garage. She made note of the car's location as she chose one of the overnight bags from the trunk and proceeded to the hotel registration area. She registered as Carol Shea providing photo identification and a VISA card under the same name.

"May I help you with your check-in?" came a Creole accent with a soft voice and pleasant smile.

"Yes, I'm Carol Shea, checking in. I have a reservation for one night," as she handed the hotel clerk her driver's license and VISA card.

"I have your reservation. You are checking in for one night, correct? "

"Yes, that's right."

"Will you need assistance with luggage or parking?"

"I'm fine with both, thanks."

"May I help you with dinner reservations, or any other of our amenities?"

"No thanks, I'm just going to get settled in my room for now."

Alex carried her small overnight bag to her room and sat in silence for fifteen minutes.

Earlier that day she had traveled from Jacksonville with a stop in the Florida panhandle to exchange cars from her own to one that had been provided for her trip to New Orleans. It was critical to not have her car in New Orleans. There could be no ties to her being in New Orleans at the time of the assassination. Arrangements for the exchange of cars were made by the unknown party financing her mission, delivered to her in a series of coded messages.

Alex left home at six o'clock in the morning. She had placed all of her supplies for the mission in the trunk of her car following her shower and a breakfast of plain yogurt and blueberries. She crumpled her two page checklist, placed it in a small plastic grocery bag, and then placed it in her car. It would be disposed of at the rest-area stop on the way to her meeting for the car exchange. The early morning departure enabled her to beat most of the morning rush-hour traffic. In less than 40-minutes, she was driving west on I-10.

"This mission is officially underway," she said loudly, trying to bring her mission into focus.

During the drive from her home in Jacksonville to the point of the car exchange, there were four and a half hours of final mental preparation for the mission with breaks to listen to some of her favorite music and motivational tapes. The second leg of the trip with the new car would be mostly silent; no personal tapes, cds, or mobile phone, only radio stations.

The first list for the mental review was the travel to the car exchange. Her review detailed one stop at a rest area for a bathroom break, choosing her morning snack, dumping the checklist and other paper and plastic items she had placed in the plastic trash bag before leaving home. Her hope was to make it to the rest stop at the I-10 exit at Florida State Road 81. On her previous planning trips she found that this rest area was ideal for her first stop. From there it was traveling farther west exit at Highway 87 then south to the Indian Nation compound near Holley. There she would be met by a representative of the tribal leader who would direct her to the place where the car exchange would take place. Participation of the tribal leader indicated how private and significant the mission was, and how significant and secret the planning and preparation had been.

Alex had never met the Tribal Chairwoman, but she had seen photos of her and heard her voice on tape. Next, Alex imagined the extensive checklist and the car exchange and the new car. A mission for an assassination isn't easy. There is little to no room for error.

Alex would mentally review this checklist three more times prior to the car exchange. During this leg of the trip, she listened to music and motivational tapes while on breaks from her mental preparation. She had prepared several for this trip. *Call Me the Breeze* was her first choice. This one was great for her since the piano player and the Lynyrd Skynyrd group was from Jacksonville, FL. There were other Skynyrd favorites. She and her friends had attended a couple of great Skynyrd events at the Jacksonville Coliseum. Plus, her sister Jena and brother Bo were both big Skynyrd fans. She had also chosen an old, but favorite motivational speaker, Jim Rohn to listen to. Rohn had been around for decades, but she had learned to take great value from his messages of discipline and motivation. One quote: *"Discipline is the bridge between goals and accomplishment"* was posted above the entry door when she taught middle school athletics.

Alex exited I-10 at the Highway 87 exit, made a quick stop at the rest area then turned south for the 20-plus miles to Holley and the compound.

Twenty-five minutes later she turned off Highway 87 onto the road leading to the Indian compound grounds. She was met by a young man, probably 12 to 14 years old. He waved for her to stop,

"Ms. Reed is over at the Council House; drive over there," as he pointed to a white building in the center of the grounds and ran ahead of Alex.

"Stay right here, I'll go get her."

At the same time a stately woman dressed in a beautiful embroidered and beaded Indian skirt and blouse motioned for Alex to stop in front of the Council House. The Tribal Chairwoman walked to the passenger side of the car and opened the passenger door, sat in the front seat and reached over and touched Alex's hand.

"Hi, I'm Amanda Reed and you are the person we are here to help with your mission."

Alex nodded, "Yes".

"Please drive over to that house and garage," pointing to a nearby residence.

"Your car is ready. Mark is there waiting to help you."

As she exited the car, the Chairwoman spoke, "This is what we were asked to do. God bless, and we are anxious to welcome you back following your success."

Alex felt like she was among spirits, and quickly obliged, seeing a man waving to her from the front porch of the house.

As Alex approached the parking area in front of the house, a thin elderly man dressed in a Levi's shirt and jeans with white hair pulled back in a ponytail motioned for her to park alongside the driveway then walked toward Alex's side of the car. As she stepped out of the car the man introduced himself.

"I am Mark, and I've been asked to help you with your other car. It's here in the garage."

Alex reached out to shake his hand. "Thank you, Mark, I appreciate your help. I'll need to move my belongings to the other car."

Mark backed the car out of the garage and parked it along side Alex's.

"When you're through I'll move your car into the garage."

After the items were moved to the exchange car, Alex spent the next five minutes going through a mental checklist which included confirming the registration and insurance matched her fictitious 'Carol Shea' driver's license and photo ID, then checking for electronic devices or "bugs." The final check included an inspection of the headlights, taillights, directional signals and anything else that might cause a police officer to stop her while she was traveling.

"Well Mark, everything looks good. Thank you so much for your help."

"May the Creator be with you," Mark replied as he turned and walked toward the Council House.

At the car exchange Alex became Carol Shea for the second leg of the mission for travel to New Orleans, the remainder of the day and evening and through the morning check-out of the Marriott.

"Ok, leg two of the mission," she said out loud as she drove past the Compound back onto Highway 87 leading to I-10 west to New Orleans.

The next four and one-half hours of travel from Holley, Florida, to New Orleans, Louisiana, Alex would focus on details of the mission, a mental check list of all the things she had studied and practiced for this mission during the past two months.

Chapter 2

Meticulous Preparation

Me-tic-u-lous *Adjective – Taking or showing extreme care about minute details; precise; thorough. – Very careful about doing something in an extremely accurate and exact way.*

Prep-a-ra-tion *Noun – The action or process of making ready or being made ready for use or consideration. Something done to get ready for an event or undertaking. The activity or process of making something ready or becoming ready for something.*

Preparation for killing a person professionally is both mental and physical to the extreme. Assassins cannot engage in hatred or jealousy. Their killing cannot be impulsive. Alex had years of training and knew that each mission had to become a well-planned obsession in order to succeed.

   This obsession comes through some strange and powerful mental chemistry. It is something that a person has developed over time. This strong desire for something they know is their life's goal; something they are destined to do. That same powerful mental chemistry does not allow their mind to recognize impossible or immoral. They are obsessed. Their brain becomes magnetized with the dominant thought. This thought attracts the forces, the people and the circumstances of life. They live with an intense desire. Meeting their goal is driven by a state of mind that is this absolute obsession. They must plan definite ways and means to achieve their goal then back these plans with persistence which does not recognize the concepts of impossibility or failure.

   Alex's teen years and early twenties were full of athletic

8

endeavors and outdoor recreational activities. She participated in high school track and field, excelling in the 440-yard run. In her high school junior year she began her long-term participation in martial arts. In her college freshman and sophomore years she was on the University of North Carolina ladies track and field team and again participated at a championship level in the 440-yard run. In addition to athletic competition, Alex enjoyed the sports of hunting and fishing, especially with her older brother Bo.

At age twenty-one, Alex was referred by a friend of her family to a person affiliated with the University of North Carolina athletic department to be considered for a new program focused on combating local terrorism. The first step in the program included the choosing of seven prospects or candidates to be tested for fitness for the program. Each of the seven was provided a fictitious name and identification for the five day mental and physical event. No one enrolled in the program knew each other's real identity. Those chosen to be offered to continue with the program would return for 30 days training at a Tennessee location. Alex was the one of seven in her group that was chosen. There were three others chosen from other groups in areas outside North Carolina.

Training was led by three Native Americans; two women and one man. They were unknown to any of the participants, again using assumed names and personal identification. The 30-day program included an intense training and practice of message receipt and delivery, physical training for stamina and coordination, the use of numerous weapons including firearms, hand-to-hand combat weapons, martial arts, and several poisonous herbal weapons.

It is a common belief among southeastern Indians that revenge killings have been a part of Indian life throughout their history. According to historian and author Charles Hudson and many others, ancestral Cherokee, Creek and other southeastern Indians have held similar beliefs and practices regarding personal wrongdoings from theft to murder. These were part of the family or clan systems. Simply put, they were "an eye for an eye" version of the Christian belief; although Christians wouldn't admit to this. Some practices and situations were determined to require different forms of retaliations; however, retaliations and revenge were deemed proper. Clan revenge or retaliation, one death revenged another and the matter was settled, at least in principal.

It was understood by all program participants that requests for a participant's services came from a group who had taken the initiative to determine what revenge situation required a killing.

In the future, if she was to participate, Alex understood, fully accepted and agreed that requests for her services would come from a group unknown to her. This group had made the determination what revenge situations required a killing.

If the prospects were chosen and they accepted they were required to assimilate into the general population with the ability to be available for missions, weekend trainings, and three years of continuing 30-days training each year. If ready and agreeable to the prospect and program directors, accompanied missions would begin the first year; lone missions would begin in the third year. Salary for each participant started at $36,000 per year. Alex was chosen and accepted.

Immediately following graduation from the University of North Carolina undergraduate studies, Alex accepted a position as a physical education instructor at an Ashville, North Carolina junior high school. Her teaching schedule provided ample time to participate in the continuing training program.

Alex's first mission was to accompany one of the Native American trainers. The mission lasted three days. The target died as a result of an herbal weapon dropped under the chair at an upscale Atlanta, Georgia, restaurant. There were two additional accompanied missions with the second one with the leader as an observer only. Each mission was a success.

Seven months later, at age 24, Alex was assigned to her first lone mission. Her victim died of a rifle shot from 40 yards. She was then removed from her annual salary and would now be paid for participation and successes with each mission. Alex had become a professional assassin.

Two years and two more successful missions later, Alex accepted a job at the University of North Florida in Jacksonville where she would teach physical education and martial arts. This too provided time and cover for her role in assassinations.

As part of each mission, Alex had learned her need to be faceless. By now her years of mission experience and continuing training made her preparation routine. Alex had been taught that being faceless while on a mission was mandatory. This is a part of her obsession. Being a Millennial, her desires were the opposite. She likes being fit and showing it; she likes bright colored clothes, she loves wearing branded goods, Under Armor and LuLu Lemon were her favorites. None of these desires can take place while on a mission.

Preparation for each mission included a dress rehearsal with outfits that met her faceless requirements from head to toe. Hair, face, eyes and eyebrows, lips; she carried one makeup, a light brown facial powder to use on her eyebrows and upper cheeks to help soften her high cheekbones and mute her brown eyes when she wasn't wearing sun glasses.

Clothing: No hats, no shorts, no tight fitting clothes, no logos, clothing colors light blue and gray, shoes non-descript plain sneakers or walking shoes. No jewelry.

Alex packed one outfit for each half-day of a mission plus four extra in case a mission required extra days. She took one or two into her room each night for use the next day. Hotel accommodations were made for one night only with each hotel registration in a different name. Each name was one of a past friend whose characteristics she knew well. It gave her comfort to be the likes of someone she knew, trusted, and liked.

This faceless practice allows her to stay focused on her mission and targets. The practice was critical when preparing for a close-up kill. The target cannot notice you. If you're outstanding in any way, your target could take note of you. During your close stalking or following, the target you often have one or more crossings or encounters, the target might recognize you or remember you as someone he or she has seen before. When "faceless" is done right, it's very difficult for any witness to remember you or describe you.

Through an unknown member or affiliate of the Eastern Cherokee Tribe, a package was delivered to Alex each year on her birthday. It contained seven items for her work. A second package delivered one week later contained a coded message for instructions on how to use each item. Often the coded message was tied to a generic cookbook available at most bookstores.

The Goetz mission was complex. The New Orleans area made it more difficult. There were a number of potential kill sites to use each with its own complexity. The daily change of location and persona needed significant planning. Preparations for this mission included her car, her clothing, and her New Orleans hotels. She had driven her car to a planned location in Holley, Florida, and exchanged it for car provided to her by an unknown entity or person. She could not take a chance of her car being spotted in New Orleans during the mission. The car registration and insurance matched one of the sets of identification carried by Alex on this trip. She had packed eight small overnight bags, two for each day. Each carried different identification, a set of clothing and accessories for the day, basic toiletries, and nutrition bars.

Defense against facial recognition security cameras requires significant attention to the eyes, nose lips, cheek bones as well as the clothing, shoes, jewelry and hair. Within the overnight bags she'll carry four pair of sunglasses, two sets of non-prescription non-colored glasses, two sets of colored contact lenses, one brown, the other hazel. Each bag contains a hat and one pair of plain converse tennis shoes, tan, light blue or white. Part of the preparation for this mission included several weeks of wearing different items to be matched then chosen for each overnight bag.

She carried a small overnight bag for toiletries and a small amount of makeup. Her daily identification included a driver's license with the photo and a second photo of a person who looked much like Alex, enough to pass any check-in, but not Alex. She also was provided credit cards with the same name. All were produced by an entity unknown to her. She had learned last year that it was likely an underground group in the San Diego, California area. She had also learned through her 14 years of training and experience to have total trust in the weaponry and identifications provided were of utmost secret and could not be traced to her. On this mission, Alex was registered, pre-paid for one night in each of four hotels. If a fifth one was necessary she would register as a walk-in. Once she was actually on a mission she didn't carry a live cell phone, not even a burner phone, but she did carry an unregistered unconnected smart phone to look the part when needed from time to time while stalking.

Weapon of first choice was a water reed three and one-half inches long one-quarter in diameter filled with a deadly mixture. It was designed for a face-to-face encounter. The "birthday" package had contained three of these. Alex brought them all for this mission.

The reed is sealed at three-eighths of an inch from one end of the reed with bees wax. The first cell contains one-half inch of dried oleander flower plus a small portion of an oleander leaf dried for three weeks then ground into a powder and placed carefully against the bees wax seal. A second seal of fine mesh was inserted and sealed again with two drops of bees wax. The second cell contained three quarters of an inch of three or four day old elm tree buds dried and ground. Two drops of venom from a female black widow spider were added to the elm tree buds. One quarter inch of powdered rose hip flowers are placed on the venom and elm tree bud. A top seal of fine mesh and bees wax was the final seal for the weapon.

The reeds were kept in a sealed container for two months before being inspected by the maker and shipped. They were tolerant of ninety degree heat up to two hours, but caution to keep them at room temperature was critical.

The reeds were to be blown with a firm puff of air at the face or neck area of the target. The upper one and one-half inches allowed for pressure from the puff of air to easily spray the target. The weapons range was up to three feet, but most effective at eighteen inches to two feet. The mixture was odorless, slightly noticeable – like light soot, and deadly. The projected mixture was designed to deliver death in two to four minutes. Alex had used the reed weapon on her last kill and found its intent accurate. She practiced the use daily with an empty reed.

Her practice and plan was to place the reed in the palm of her hand, close the palm into a fist, aim and blow. She preferred using the left hand so an approach from the right side of the target facing her was best.

The other killing weapons included a vial with similar content that was dropped at the foot of a person sitting, a poison used by placing it in a drink and third, a larger vial designed to be placed in a room while the target was sleeping. She owned two firearms for use, but a long-range rifle and short range pistol were not appropriate for use on this mission.

Preparations for this mission included a full month of studying the target, Goetz, his life style, his work place, his background and his home. It included two visits to the site of his work and home areas prior to the month of study. Alex was provided a number of photos of Goetz which she had destroyed prior to the trip. She had seen him at a distance a handful of times, from a few yards away once and nearly face-to-face twice on previous visits. Her month away from the site prior to the mission would avoid any familiarity of Goetz or other potential witnesses, and any street or building cameras. The site visits enabled her to study the streets and buildings that would be or could be involved. Site visits also included a sighting and noting as such items as street and building cameras, restaurants with various street, walkway and sidewalk views, and becoming comfortable with a number of scenarios for the kill. All of her information was committed to memory avoiding outside access to a data site or written notes left in a room, her car or on her possession.

Preliminary work including previous on-site visits to the area had yielded six sites that were believed to have the best potential for this type of kill with the least amount of risk to her physically and the least likely to provide police or other authorities of witnesses and photos by street cameras. Her notes for the six sites are provided below:

Goetz Kill Sites, revised –

1. *Doubletree Hotel bldg . Staying at Doubletree Hotel 4th night. - overlooking the rear Canal/St.Peters Street casino entry/exit. WOW restaurant, first floor Doubletree. Not a good or acceptable kill site. OK for sighting Goetz' entry or exit. Not possible to take action if he is sighted, plus Goetz is not known to use or visit.*

2. *Café du Monde and Washington Square. Jackson Square directly across the street. Goetz frequents here so good place to sight. Often meets people here. Across the intersection from his apartment complex. OK to consider kill here, but limited. Best to spot him, leave ahead of him, wait across the intersection [caution street/intersection surveillance cameras]. Wait at ground floor Pontalba retail area then take action on his exit from du monde to his apartment.*

3. *Café Pontalba at first floor of Pontalba building overlooking Jackson Square and the St. Louis Cathedral entry. Best view is from the intersection area or inside the fencing of Jackson sq. Goetz known to frequent here for eat and drinks – meets lady friends since his apartment is on the second floor of the building. Good site for sighting, possible, but difficult for kill site.*

4. *Gumbo Pot restaurant outdoor fenced area overlooking Trolley stop at Toulouse Street (Jax Brewery). Route most used by Goetz to and from Harrah's/Canal Street entrance. From inside the fenced outdoor patio area, good sighting spot, but impossible to get out in time to affect a close-up kill. Best to practice and consider being at the Trolley stop/shelter for a shot at Goetz between the Trolley stop and Decatur Street area of Toulouse Street for Goetz's trip to work or trip from work. Practice this one a few more times.*

5. *Fulton Street and Fulton Alley – At Gordon Biersch outdoor seats/tables or Ruth Chris outdoor. Breakfast – need to purchase muffin at the bakery stand in escalator area entry to Harrah's or use other seating between entry and Fulton – bowling alley. Good for morning or evening sighting if Goetz is still in a relationship with Fulton Alley lady manager. Kill area is within the walking area between the bowling alley and entry and Ruth Chris-Gordon Biersch area. Caution with street cameras. Should be able to avoid street cameras...quite far apart.*

6. *Hilton Hotel Riverwalk –seating at Drago's overlooking Poydres Street and intersection. Goetz does visit the second floor café for meetings with people- near the hotel registration area. Goetz also stops for lunch and after-hour drinks at Drago's and the first floor restaurant. Good sighting site, possible kill site. Second part of site is the Riverwalk retail area and food court. Extensive area but Goetz is known to stroll here with his lady friends.*

Hotels – Night one, Marriott on Canal Street as Carol Shea/Night two, French Market Inn as Nancy Beaudoin/Night three, Provincial Hotel as Nancy Cole/Night four Doubletree as Georgian Ringland. If longer repeat one thru four. Spent time at each one on previous trips. Best of nine reviewed for work there. Park car at the Marriott open parking for the four nights since parking is difficult at the other sites. Avoid open parking at Harrah's.

Preparation for financial arrangements for each mission was made several weeks prior; this was no exception. All financial arrangements were made by Alex's sister, Jena.

Jena spoke and wrote fluent Cherokee from the Sequoia syllabary. All communications were made in code using the Cherokee symbols. Verbal communications were not allowed. Fees were made by a pre-determined plan for the believed complexity and difficulty of the mission. Fees consisted of eighty percent precious metals and coins; twenty percent cash. Initial upfront fees were sent to Jena's dance studio in packages with return labels of dance-wear and music stores. Once the fee arrangements were made, Jena would remove herself from knowing further details. From this point all communications regarding the mission were communicated to Alex in various coded messages from unknown persons. There were four codes for acceptance of communication to and from followed by a second code using symbols from the Cherokee syllabary.

Receipt of payment for missions was again the sole responsibility of Jena. Twenty percent of the fee was delivered to Jena at the completion of the arrangements. An additional thirty percent was delivered to Jena at the time Alex departed on her mission. Alex would deliver her departure message by code to the unknown party responsible for delivering the payment. The final fifty percent was delivered upon completion of the mission. These payments were delivered by courier to a specific partner at a large law firm in Winston-Salem, North Carolina to be held in coded names in the law firm's vault. Alex and Jena met with the attorney twice each year.

All preparations required meticulous and cautious planning and actions. Above her exercise facility office door was a quote she lived by:

"We must all suffer one of two things; the pain of discipline or the pain of regret." - Jim Rohn.

Chapter 3

The Hunt Continues – The First Sighting and Surprise

The Marriott Hotel on Canal Street was the one chosen for her first night stay based on her previous visits to New Orleans in preparation for this mission. Alex had designated Café du Monde the first stop for sighting her target.

Following her arrival in New Orleans and check-in at the hotel, she sat in silence in her room. As she broke from her silence, Alex thought to herself "Ok, I'm here, checked in, I can finish my preparation for yoga and meditation, then ready to go."

Alex's daily routine included yoga and meditation, usually sometime between late morning and early afternoon. During this mission it would most likely be when changing from one hotel to the next. Today it will be following her check-in, prior to her work this afternoon and evening. Typically, her daily routine included a morning jog or run. Today her early travel didn't allow her the luxury.

August 11, 2015, 4:25 pm

"Ok, yoga, let's stretch, regenerate some energy," as she began her routine.

Following yoga was her twenty plus minute meditation. Alex had practiced this routine for over seven years. It was an integral part of her life; more demanding while on a mission.

An hour and fifteen minutes after arriving at the hotel she was ready for her afternoon and evening work.

5:40 pm

Alex exited her room and headed down the hallway. It's a three minute walk from the hotel, and two blocks from my kill site for this evening.

Café du Monde was one of six pre-determined sites for the mission. Alex had labeled it as "KILL SITE 2." Her notes created during research for the mission read:

> KILL SITE 2 – *Café du Monde and Washington Square. Jackson Square directly across the street. Goetz frequents here so good place to sight. Often meets people here. Across the intersection from his apartment complex. OK to consider kill here, but limited. Best to spot him, leave ahead of him, wait across the intersection [caution street/intersection surveillance cameras]. Wait at ground floor Pontalba retail area then take action on his exit from du monde to his apartment.*

Alex determined this was the best early evening site to spot her target, Kevin Goetz. He was known to often meet with people here in the early, pre-dinner hours. A sighting tonight would give Alex a reassurance that he was in New Orleans, as expected, and a sighting would give her a great boost of confidence that her mission and her planning would result in success. A kill would complete her mission.

She sat in silence again reviewing the plan for the evening; clothes, weapons, her mental picture of her target, her route, and her seating at Café du Monde.

"I'm on my way," she said out loud as she took three deep breaths on her way out the door like an athlete stepping onto the field for the start of a championship game.

"Ok, Carol Shea. This is it. Focus. Be patient," she reminded herself.

5:52 pm

Alex seated herself at a table in the left rear of the Cafe where she had a good view of all the seating. Her research and preparation for this mission details that her target visits here often for evening meetings with friends and business associates.

She had visited New Orleans before, once as a tourist with friends and two times before on business, to detail her plans to kill Kevin Goetz. She had studied the tourist in New Orleans on her previous trips to feel comfortable in that role and appear as part of the crowd.

6:16 pm

"There he is," she thought to herself. "Just stay calm, see what happens. See who he meets. See what he's doing here."

Alex checked her handbag for her weapons. Tonight she carried two weapons. Both were secure. Tonight she was dressed in her dress-down look with hair down, oversized faded long sleeved plaid cotton shirt and Levis; always neutral colors, no logos, no bright colors, nothing identifiable. No makeup, no jewelry; plain light blue cotton sneakers.

She recognized him from her previous visits and the extensive detail which had been provided to her by someone unknown to her. Tonight he was neatly dressed in a dark grey suit with a great looking necktie.

"Overboard conservative look," she whispered to herself again.

Goetz sat five tables away from Alex. Tables at Café du Monde were close to each other. Not much room to get around. Alex stayed seated showing her right side. Her seating plan was correct. She did not want to be facing him to avoid having him see her face front on. She needed to avoid having any future recognition of her. Her final move would likely require a close up shot or drop so she couldn't afford to have the slightest chance of recognition. She was able to have glancing looks at him.

"I might be able to hear some of a conversation if he meets with someone," she thought to herself, "but that's not why I'm here right now. Don't be eager……Be patient," she reminded herself. "Be patient."

A few minutes later Goetz was waving to a man dressed in a

casual sport coat and slacks motioning for him to come over to his table. They met with a hearty handshake and smiles.

"Who is this? Pakistani or Indian maybe?" she thought as she tried to get a good look at the man.

Goetz had been the Assistant General Manager at Harrah's Cherokee Casino for three years. The Cherokee Tribe had suspected him of skimming and had openly threatened him. Harrah's manages the casino for the Eastern Band of Cherokee Tribe and had investigated Goetz but couldn't prove the accusations. Harrah's was now owned by Caesars Entertainment and was known to move managers around often. Caesars was in financial trouble and couldn't afford further negative publicity. He was now an Assistant General Manager of Harrah's in New Orleans under the close scrutiny of a seasoned casino manager.

Alex didn't know any of the individuals who had hired her. There was never a direct contact. She believed it was someone or some group associated with the Tribe or Caesars. It was her practice to not know.

"Just stick with the basics right now," she told herself. "I've found him; my research is working, lay low for now. I just got here," she reminded herself. "I've found Goetz, lay low right now. I can't hear their conversation. See if I can figure out who this other person is; follow him tonight and make plans for tomorrow morning." Her mind was running with ideas.

Alex checked her handbag again to be sure her weapons were ok. "Ok, be ready when an opportunity comes. Woah, this is just the first hour." She caught herself staring at the two men.

"Back off, don't look directly at them….don't stare" she scolded.

Her pulse had elevated with the sighting and the thought. She took a small book from her handbag and pretended to read or look at a brochure map.

The waiter brought her beignets heaped with powdered sugar

along with coffee and ice water. The beignets and coffee gave her a way to relax for a few minutes. It distracted her and made her feel like a New Orleans tourist. "Carol Shea did and still does make a good tourist," she thought with a slight smile.

"Who is this guy?" she asked herself. Alex was just out of hearing range plus all the noise of New Orleans and the French Quarter made it impossible to hear any of their conversation. Her guess was they were discussing their work.

"Do they work together?"She considered to herself. "I really need to find out who this is"

She was ready to leave to sit outside and follow Goetz when he left the Café, but her instincts told her to stay...to see if there was anything else she could learn about what was going on between the two. She cautiously listened and watched for anything that would provide a clue as to who this guy was and what the two were doing here. "Hold back, don't leave yet. Take another bite of beignet, another sip of coffee, a few more sips of water. Be patient. Just give it a few more minutes," she thought to herself.

"Watch and listen," she told herself.

She waited and watched to see if there was any paperwork, or exchange of notes or business cards.

"Nothing, just a fairly intense, yet friendly conversation." The waiters knew Goetz, brought him an iced tea, while the stranger had ice water.

A few minutes later Alex left her seat and table to move to a spot outside the Café at a bench across the street, on the sidewalk outside Jackson Square where she could see the men leave, then follow Goetz. Her research detailed that he lived across the street at the Pontalba Apartments overlooking Jackson Square.

"I'll see where this guy goes, but I need to keep my focus on Goetz," she reminded herself. Alex had never seen or heard of this person. Her previous visits and all the research she had been provided didn't describe or name anyone of his description.

6:55 pm

The calliope on the steamboat Natchez started playing its music to begin its departure for the evening cruise. It was part of the New Orleans excitement and charm. The music always caught the attention of tourists visiting New Orleans. Alex smiled as she watched them scurry to get closer to the steamboat paddlewheel.

7:09 pm

Goetz and his meeting partner left Café du Monde and separated at the intersection. Goetz crossed the street to the Pontalba Apartments; his friend stayed on the Café du Monde side of the street and walked north toward Harrah's Casino. Alex waited to see Goetz enter the apartment building. Her attention turned to the stranger. He was gone from her sight.

"Who is this guy?"

She turned her attention back to Goetz.

"Dammit, I think I just missed an opportunity," she said out loud. "If I'd been awake, I would have been at the corner at the Pontalba and hit Goetz there. It would be over. Dammit. What a rookie mistake. Dammit. Why did I do that? She thought to herself.

"Come on Cowart, you're better than that. Total, total, focus. Total focus on the mission. This isn't your first mission," she reminded herself again.

After scolding herself and taking half a dozen deep breaths, she crossed the street and sat on the steps of Washington Square facing Jackson Square for a few minutes then moved to the top of the square to view the beautiful Mississippi River.

"Ok, go back to the hotel; get my brains back in my head."

A large southbound ship drifted by making the turn at the crescent. She listened to the quiet steady beat of its engines as it made the turn. She could stay here for hours and watch the ships and people. She reminded herself that this has to be one of the greatest places in the world to sit, watch, listen and imagine. As she was gathering herself to leave for the evening, Alex saw a little of red color in the early sunset. Tomorrow should be a good day.

As she got ready to leave Washington Square to walk back to her room, she looked for someone to walk close to, preferably someone fairly well dressed. "It's getting dark. Avoid the creeps," she reminded herself.

Just as she was leaving, she sat back down on the concrete steps, and she remembered her first trip to New Orleans at age 22. She had been with two of her friends, Erika Yates, a co-worker, and Carol Shea, an ex- college roommate, the person whose name she was currently using. It was a trip to celebrate Erika's birthday. Alex remembered it like it was yesterday. On the car ride to New Orleans that day Erika and Carol were giddy about going to Bourbon Street. Alex could still hear Carol say, "We've got to go to Bourbon Street at night. We just have to go."

The first evening there they walked on North Peters street toward Jackson Square. After watching the street entertainment in front of St. Peters Cathedral they had dinner at the Pontalba restaurant, and then walked a few blocks to Bourbon Street.

As soon as they reached the infamous street and its crowd, Alex blurted out "Bunch of freaks."

Carol replied, "Yea, but it's fun. It's Bourbon Street; we have to see it,"

Erika agreed. "Let's just stay a little longer. Then we can go back to Jackson Square."

As they turned to go back into the Bourbon Street crowd, two men put beads around their necks, uttered a few profanities as one of the men groped Erika, the other groped Alex aggressively. Alex reacted with a sweeping upward motion striking him directly in the nostrils with the butt of her open hand.

"Get your hands off me you son-of-bitch," she blurted out as she struck him.

Alex had reacted out of fear and survival just as she had been trained to do.

"Aaaugh…Aaaugh" he shouted, blood spraying like a faucet from his nose through his fingers as he held his hand over his face and fell to the ground gasping for air.

A dozen or more people surrounded the scene as the man screamed and pain and contorted his body on the ground now with a pool of blood starting to form.

At the same time Erika and Carol had scratched, kicked and screamed curse words, names and phrases at the other man, sounds and words no one in the crowd had likely heard before.

"Let's get the Hell out of here" Alex yelled out as she kicked the second man in the groin then struck him in the side of the knee, caving the knee sideways, likely tearing the muscle and ligaments. He too went down to the ground grasping and holding his knee and crotch screaming in pain.

The stunned crowd didn't move, only yelled out "Get an ambulance!" and "Hurry!"

Erika, Carol and Alex looked at each other as they ran away from the crowd in front of the Cathedral into the crowd walking between the Pontalba Apartments and Jackson Square. Erika knew her way back to the hotel and guided the other two to the Washington Square and the crowd at the Café du Monde corner. They stopped long enough to catch their breath, regroup and walk the five blocks back to the hotel.

25

The sounds of sirens came from the Bourbon Street area.

Once in the room, Erika broke down and cried hysterically into one of the pillows on the bed. Carol and Alex held back tears.

An hour later with the trembling and shock partially over, Alex suggested they leave the next morning. She knew that the might have killed the first man and that the second man would likely need extensive leg and knee surgery.

"God, Alex, you really hurt them both. Where did you ever learn to do that?"

Before Alex could respond, Carol spoke out, "The jerks deserved it, whatever happened, they deserved it. Alex, I'm impressed with what you did. I'm still shocked by it…. but boy am I impressed."

"Thanks. I wish I didn't have to do it. I just reacted, that's all. I just reacted. And I'm glad, too."

She paused, took a deep breath, "I'm glad I did it."

The memory was still vivid as she focused back on her mission. "That was 10 years ago and I'm still glad I could do it and I'm still glad I did it," she said out loud to herself.

"I probably killed the first man," she said to herself. "I wonder if Carol and Erika think I killed him." After all the years, the three were still friends. They never discussed the incident again with Alex.

Alex got her mind back into the mission. As she left Washington Square to return to her hotel room on the first night of her mission she realized Goetz would likely be her second victim in New Orleans. She was ready for it.

Alex walked in silence back to her hotel among an older, well-dressed crowd. From packing for the trip, the first half of the trip with mental preparation, the car exchange, the second half of the trip with mental preparation, and the stalking of Goetz, she reminded herself, "today has been long and successful."

She reminded herself, "take care of the business at hand." On her first evening of the mission, she had located Goetz. Her planning had paid off.

"But who was this other person? What were they discussing?"

The walk back to the hotel was refreshing with a slight breeze, the excitement of the streets of New Orleans. She breathed deeply as she walked.

Alex had taught herself to work with hypnotized focus. This mission needed that absolute state of mind. She could hear her heart beat and her steps over the sound of the New Orleans night life as she walked in focused silence.

Her day ended with getting ready for bed, making meticulous mental notes about tomorrow:

"My jogging route, confirm notes for street cameras from previous trips, breakfast plans – confirm plans to spot Goetz, check out of the hotel, move or leave car here, clothing and ID, name change for tomorrow after checking out of the hotel, weapons for tomorrow,11:00 am and after plans – determine early lunch site."

Her final move before going to bed was a physical review of weapons to carry tomorrow. Everything had to be right!

Chapter 4

Goetz and Friend

Self-im-por-tance Noun – *Having an exaggerated sense of one's own value or importance; pompously conceited or haughty.*

Ar-ro-gance Noun – *An attitude of superiority manifested in an overbearing manner or presumptuous claims or assumptions.*

Con-ceit Noun – *Excessive pride on one's self, ability, importance.*

Alex's search and investigations during the six months prior to the mission had provided significant details regarding the target, Kevin Goetz. Goetz is a 43-year old whose entire professional career has been in the casino and hotel industry. He attended the Columbia University School of Hotel, Restaurant and Institutional Management then completed his graduate studies in Casino Management at University of Nevada Las Vegas.

Goetz was born in the Cleveland, Ohio area where he lived until attending undergraduate studies at Columbia. He is the youngest of three children with one brother and one sister. His brother, John, the oldest, is a successful medical doctor living in the Cleveland area. His sister, Kathy, a CPA, works for a Wall Street firm in New York City. Their father, Daniel Goetz, worked in middle then upper management with the Shell Oil Company and during Kevin's youth and high school years he was employed at the Shell Oil Company Great Lakes District Oil Terminal in Cleveland. Their mother worked at AT&T after Kevin was nine years old.

According to notes provided to Alex, Kevin learned to live an active social life from his parents. His brother, John, and sister, Kathy, were less social. The family had a comfortable, trouble-free life eventually living in an upper middle class suburban Cleveland neighborhood. Kevin enjoyed summer camp at a Lake Erie summer camp and resort and participated in Little League Baseball with several of his neighborhood friends in his early years. In middle school and high school, he was active in the music programs and acting, and he was on the school baseball teams. It was also noted that he didn't have much success in baseball.

Notes provided further that Goetz was an above average middle school and high school student which, along with some influence from his father's friends, enabled him to be accepted at Columbia. The school of hotel, restaurant and institutional management and the Columbia lifestyle and social life fit him well.

Kevin married Lynda Williams, a UNLV classmate a year after completing his graduate studies. Lynda was a native of Nevada and worked as a financial advisor for Morgan Stanley in Las Vegas. She was hoping to work into the business with her father and uncle who had built their book of business for over two decades. Immediately following UNLV graduate studies, Kevin was hired by MGM in Las Vegas and enrolled into their management program where he spent 18-months.   He was transferred from Las Vegas to the MGM Grand in Detroit soon after the training period. Lynda did not relocate with him. It didn't work out. They were divorced three years after the marriage.

Notes provided also detailed his work experience in Detroit. He remained single. He had been transferred to MGM Detroit six months prior to the opening of the new Detroit facility and had enjoyed the challenge of being part of the management team during its inception and growth. A Michigan voter referendum provided for three Las Vegas style casinos to be built and operated in Detroit in an attempt to cut off the outflow of Michigan monies being spent at the Harrah's casino in Windsor, Ontario, Canada, just across the river from Detroit. MGM was chosen as one of the three. The rest of the casinos in Michigan were Indian owned.

Alex had been provided a significant amount of information about Goetz from information provided to Harrah's regarding his work and time in Detroit. Apparently Goetz had adapted well to Detroit. His early life in Cleveland was spent in slush and snow in the winter and the midwest mix of industrial companies and mid-western culture suited his social life.

While in Detroit he lived in an apartment in the Greektown area near another Detroit casino. Comerica Park, the home of the Tigers, Ford Field, home of the Detroit Lions, and Joe Lewis Arena, home of the Red Wings NHL hockey team, were all within walking distance of his apartment. Night spots and restaurants such as the Pegasus were local night life for the sports enthusiasts and frequent visits from the athletes. It appears that his love for sports was fulfilled while in Detroit. It also appears that it became a problem. MGM had noted in his file that *These sports and night-life attractions became a frequent distraction to his work."*

In addition to MGM, Detroit has two other major casino-hotel complexes, Greektown and Motor City. Greektown was owned and operated by the Sault Ste. Marie Chippewa Indians and Motor City was owned and operated by the Iliach family, owners of the Tigers and Red Wings franchises. It was noted that Goetz had likely tried more than once to go to work for the Motor City Casino.

Goetz left MGM and Detroit in 2003. In spite of his distractions, his five years with MGM had given him huge experience in a mid-sized facility with an ever-challenging environment. Goetz was hired by Harrah's first in Tunica, Mississippi as an Assistant Casino Manager where he was employed for three years. He was then transferred by Harrah's and joined the Harrah's management team in Cherokee, North Carolina Tribe as an Assistant Facilities Manager for the Casino and Hotel. Harrah's Cherokee was considered one of the best facilities and operations in the southeast. Two years later he was unexpectedly transferred to Harrah's New Orleans, another huge facility and operation, but his role was reduced to one of two Assistant managers at the Casino.

From notes and information gathered by and for Alex, it appears that Tunica, Mississippi and Cherokee, North Carolina were not to his liking as was Detroit. Notes describe each transfer with Harrah's as a career opportunity. His work at each was as acceptable to very good. Cherokee was an ideal career move and his background with MGM in Detroit made him an outstanding member of the management team. It was the other part of his life that was troubling.

He outspokenly did not like fishing, hunting, kayaking or other outdoor activities like winter skiing. The local sports bars appear to have been beneath him. Plus, Harrah's managers were cautioned about too much night life at area bars and clubs. The Carolina Panthers football team was 180 miles away, Atlanta was 160 miles away. He lived in a nice, but old, single family home 12 miles from the casino complex. Goetz had constantly complained about the "non-existent" night life although the casino and hotel complex provided an ample supply of friendly female employees.

Goetz was suspected of 'skimming' form Harrah's Cherokee during the time he was employed there. Investigations had never developed sufficient proof to formally accuse Goetz. It was possible that it was done by someone or some group from outside the organization, however it had been determined that it was most likely internal with more than one person involved. The accounting and audit department uncovered discrepancies including inconsistent credit card fee rates credited to the hotel, Harrah's Players' card fees charged to the Cherokee Tribe by Harrah's, and rental fees paid to Harrah's from restaurants within the casino and hotel complex. Each one was a fraction of one percent, but when done on large dollar volumes the dollar amounts were significant. This type of work would have required the expertise of a data processing or accounting person, most likely part of the Harrah's staff.

The 'skimmed' monies were traced to at least three named Cherokee accounts, yet the monies received by the accounts were never transferred to the Cherokee Tribe of any of its affiliates or to Harrah's. The monies were transferred through the accounts to unknown financial institutions or depositories.

Suspicion of Goetz was based on a number of factors including his comments to more than one Harrah's junior officers or managers that, "If you're going to launder money or hide money, have it go to your law firm, not your bank. The law requires bankers to report money laundering, clients of law firms are protected by attorney-client privilege." The reality is that law firms can transfer monies to off-shore or domestic financial institutions. Second, Goetz boasted of having significant amounts of money and his luxury condo in the Miami, Aventura area known for its wealthy residents and patrons. There was suspicion of dealing with drugs, but no proof was provided. The final signal of his suspected involvement was that it had started about six months after the beginning of his employment at Harrah's Cherokee and had stopped almost immediately after. No person in data processing or accounting was singled out as being a part of the scheme.

On the two previous visits to New Orleans to plan this mission, Alex traced and physically followed Goetz to his second floor apartment at the famous Upper Pontalba Building on the north side across the street from Jackson Square and across the intersection from Café du Monde. His is one of the sixteen apartment units in the building. There is an identical building on the south side of Jackson Square. Her research, more out of curiosity about the Jackson Square area, discovered that the 180 year old buildings are among the most historically and architecturally famous structures in New Orleans. The street level first floor have retail units, the second floor of each building has efficiency one and two bedroom units. Goetz unit is a one bedroom.

Over and over her preparation for the kill had discovered how huge a sports fan Kevin is. Nearly all of his friendships have some element of sports involved. She learned that during the last two years all of his vacations and breaks from work have been to horse racing events. His winter/spring breaks have been to Fort Lauderdale/Miami where he is a frequent visitor to Calder, Gulfstream Park, Hialeah and Pompano. The great part of this is that each of the four now has a casino attached. Another draw for Goetz is that Miami is one of the few cities in the U.S. with all four major league sports teams, football, baseball, hockey and basketball, plus baseball spring training.

Alex noted to herself that New Orleans provided the New

Orleans Saints; LSU and their phenomenal college teams were a little more than an hour away. For his local fix on horses he has the Fair Grounds horse racing and casino fifteen minutes from his work. Churchill Downs took over the failing facility and have made it a great place to visit on race day, plus they have a great upper-end small group meeting and banquet area that is out of the mainstream. Great for his type of get together. The management team and senior service personnel at the Fair Grounds knows Goetz and welcomes him. He's treated like a celebrity and, Alex noted: "of course, he probably loves it."

Alex pictures Goetz as having a Gatsby personality fantasy with his wardrobe, his look, his love of wealth. She could see him wearing spats. His work habits include not staying late and never taking work home. His female relationships all fit the life style of no commitment, always ready for a party, and *I really do like myself* attitude and demeanor.

Alex had to remind herself, "Be careful about being too judgmental or have beliefs or feelings about any target. Don't lose sight of the mission." She had been trained to stay away from it; it was like trying to multi-task. It doesn't work in this line of business.

Alex had never seen or heard of this person. Her previous visits and all the research she had been provided didn't name or describe anyone like him.

While on a mission Alex did not carry her own cell phone and the use of any online equipment was prohibited. It was far too easy for someone to pick up messages or key words used in research. The discipline of someone stalking to kill someone was not just high level - it was astronomical. It was especially difficult for someone who had grown up the last decade with instant messaging and research capability.

"Lay low," she reminded herself.

Chapter 5

Day Two – Fulton Street Fumble

The practice of meditation involves any activity that keeps the attention pleasantly anchored in the present moment. It calms the body through the relaxation response and fixes the mind through dropping the anchor of attention. It is the most important tool of self-healing and self-regulation.

By teaching the mind to become aware and then let go, meditation trains us in responsibility and control. By allowing the emergence of new attitudes, we develop the understanding that life's threats are better dealt with as challenges.

August 12th, 2015

A skilled professional almost always awakes with an excitement, ready to reach his or her goal. There might need to be an adjustment based on new realities, but the dream or goal is in the direct line of sight. Today, Alex's first thought was spoken out loud:

"Today should be the day. My plan is in place, I'm one hundred percent ready for this. Just be patient, trust your plan, Alex, trust your plan."

Her body and mind went directly into her morning routine; total focus on her morning run and details of her plans for the day. Today Alex finished getting dressed for her morning workout. It was a light jog-walk over to the river area starting at the hotel area then south to Washington Square and back.

"Weather is clear, no distractions, and red sky last night, this should be a great day," she reminded herself as she reviewed her morning plan over and over.

Back at her room at the Marriott, Alex showered and dressed for the day as she fought off thoughts about Mom and Jena.

"Mom will probably call Jena today. Mom gets nervous when she calls two or three days and I don't answer. Jena knows I can't call anyone while I'm on a mission."

She was a master of covering for Alex. Jena was the only one who knew a little about Alex's business, and that they were times when Alex was unavailable. Jena also knew that the minute Alex could contact her she would.

Jena and Alex had developed a phenomenal level of patience over each of their lifetimes. They had mastered patience by following their mother's example.

Mom had explained to her children the values of courage, inner strength, and patience would come largely from difficult times, like the death of her husband leaving the family in the prime of his life. His new job with the police force had given him new confidence and pride.

"Patience and courage will come from your belief in our Creator," she would say, "It will come from your love and appreciation of our ancestors."

All three children were taught these values throughout their lives living with mom. Alex and Bo talked frequently of these lessons from Mom and that they believed people of the real Cherokee spirit had these strengths, that these strengths were growing stronger each generation, not weaker. Alex and Bo told the tales and stories of the strength, courage and patience to

Jena's children whenever they could visit them.

Patience was a strength Mom taught Jena and Bo when their Dad died. It was a masterful lesson taught by example. Patience was taught by her belief in her Creator, by her pride and joy in each of her children. Mom reminded every adult she knew,

"Teach your children the love of their Creator; teach them the strength and courage of their ancestors, and teach them that patience is a great gift from our Cherokee spirits and Creator."

To have been taught the value and strength of having patience while on a mission was an enormous benefit. This would be one of those days! In addition to lessons from Mom, Uncle Kent's stories of courage and patience would always remain with Alex. Uncle Kent believes patience is a weapon. His stories of "lying face up in a rice field in Viet Nam breathing through a ½ inch reed while the enemy walked past was the ultimate test. You risked your life and the lives of your entire unit if you failed." To Uncle Kent, "water boarding is for sissies."

Alex completed her early routine and was on her short walk from the Marriott on Canal Street to Fulton Street. She kept a close eye on everything as she passed three entry/exit areas of the casino.

"The entries are fertile grounds, but too large to cover and too many cameras. I can only cover one at a time, then, if I spot him it's too hard to be where I can get a face-to-face shot. The odds are really against me here. This mission can't be done with a firearm. It's got to be close up."

Alex target place this morning was Fulton Street, across the street from the casino and adjacent to the Harrah's Hotel. Alex had designated this as Kill Site 5, per her notes:

Fulton Street and Fulton Alley – At Gordon Biersch outdoor
seats/tables or Ruth Chris outdoors. Breakfast – need to
purchase muffin at bakery stand in escalator area entry to
Harrah's or use other seating between entry and Fulton –
bowling alley. Good morning or evening sighting if Goetz
is still in a relationship with Fulton Alley lady manager. Kill
area is within the walking area between the bowling area
entry and the Ruth Chris-Gordon Biersch outdoor areas.
Caution with street cameras. Good that they are quite far
apart.

Alex's study and research for the mission describes Fulton
Street as a former city street now closed to auto and truck traffic
and used as a pedestrian retail and restaurant area. Restaurant
outdoor patios line both sides of the former roadway. Gordon
Biersch and Ruth Chris are the most notable. Walking traffic is a
mix of locals and tourist.

Alex had spent time surveying the area with special scrutiny of
security cameras. Some cameras are now used for facial
recognition, so extreme caution with sites like this and the other
five she had surveyed on her previous visits are necessary. She
discovered two areas in the Fulton Street area that were outside
of the camera view where any killing would have to take place.
Alex reminded herself about her preparation; Defense against
facial recognition requires attention to the eyes, nose and lips as
well as clothing items, shoes rings and other jewelry and hair.

Alex was an expert at this, including four pair of sunglasses,
two sets of non-prescription glasses, two sets of colored contact
lenses along with numerous hats and hairpieces, no jewelry, three
pair of plain different colored tan, white and light blue converse
tennis shoes. Plans for use of each were chosen and packed in her

daily overnight bags prior to leaving on a mission.

Alex knew Goetz would often walk the few blocks on Fulton Street to meet with one of his favorite lady friends who managed the Fulton Street Bowling Alley and Grill. Alex walked casually from the front entrance gate of Fulton Street back to a block past the bowling alley entrance then began to retrace her route.

"This is a good place to be," she said out loud to herself. She was fully ready with two weapons, the blow-reed and a drop package.

8:40 am

A woman who Alex believed could be Goetz's lady friend was walking through the entrance walking toward Alex. As they passed each other, Alex moved to have a better view.

"Yea, that's her," Alex thought as the woman unlocked the entry door to the bowling area.

8:47 am

Alex had found a seat away from the walking traffic and security camera coverage near the bowling alley waiting hopefully for Goetz to arrive.

"I see him; this is it," she whispered to herself.

"Ok, he's coming toward me; get on my left, his right, and weapon ready."

She walked as casually as possible to the center of walking traffic and headed toward Goetz who was in full stride. With the blow reed in her left hand she started her countdown, "5 -4 – 3- 2- aim, blow!"

Suddenly, a man jumped in front of Goetz.

"What the Hell!" she yelled out.

A man had run between the two and likely took the load in the side of the face or head. Everything stopped.

"What the Hell did you do," she yelled at the man.

"Get the Hell out of here," she told herself. She quickly saw that the man was falling to the ground, taking all the attention from her and Goetz.

Goetz yelled out, "Hey lady, hey you, what just happened?"

The wife of the victim screamed, "Robert, Robert, get up! Help, Help."

A man's voice was heard, "Somebody call an ambulance. This man is having a heart attack," came more than one yell from the crowd surrounding the scene with the man lying on the ground.

Alex quickly realized that the man had been trying to catch his son who had run to the other side of the alley.

The lady and young boy ran to the fallen man. "Somebody help! Get up, Robert, Get Up!" the lady screamed hysterically.

"Dad, Dad, get up!" yelled the son.

Alex gathered her wits, "Ok, regroup, get the hell out of here" as she walked as casually as possible toward the entry gate on her way back to the Marriott.

"Don't look back; don't rush; re-group – re-group," she reminded herself.

"Dammit, there are street cameras all over the place...What the hell just happened? I think I just killed a man, and not my target, not Goetz."

Within five minutes, the block was swarmed with police cars and an ambulance.

"Maybe I missed him; maybe the load hit him on the side of the head, maybe in the back of the head; maybe he's not dead. Ok, keep calm, regroup. Dammit, I hope Goetz didn't see the shot or see me. Dammit, just get a grip; get back to my room, remember the mission, deep breaths. Ok, don't look back; don't hurry; re-group. Remember my mission," she reminded herself as she walked nervously past the Harrah's Hotel, out of Fulton Street then the casino then to her hotel.

"Ok, back to the room. Relax, look casual" she reminded herself as she walked through the Marriott lobby to the elevator.

Once in the room, Alex made sure all the door locks were locked then went straight to the bathroom, and looked at herself in the mirror and took five deep belly-breaths.

"I had him" she said out loud, "I had him," she said a second time as she lay on the bed.

"Get my mind back in control," she said out loud as she held her hands on the side of her head. "Stay right here, regroup. Don't go back there right now."

Thirty minutes later her instincts and training had enabled Alex to calm down and regroup. "Ok, it's nine twenty-five; I'll go for a second run, hit the hotel fitness center, come back up here and get my plan for the rest of the day in order."

In a few minutes she was on the hotel elevator on her way for a run along the Mississippi riverfront.

Her run started at the Aquarium toward the French Market.

"This will be an entirely different crowd that Fulton Street," Alex assured herself. "I need to get this morning out of my mind. This is great, the river walk people are so different from other parts of New Orleans," she said aloud as she pushed her run faster and harder southward along the river.

She ran past Waldenberg Park, past Washington Square past the French Market.

"Wow, this feels good. Ok, back to the Marriott fitness center, change outfits. Crap, I've got to go to the car for a different outfit. It's got to be totally different. Ok, to the car, then to the fitness center. Ok, it's nine fifty-five now, to the car; to the fitness center, shower and change, meditation, check out of the hotel, lunch, be back on the hunt by eleven thirty-five."

Alex finished her run, back to the room for the car keys; pick up the second outfit, back to the room to leave the car keys and second outfit, and then back down the elevator to the exercise room. She worked out for twenty minutes on an elliptical then back to the room for a shower.

"Ok, ten twenty-eight, I've got my half-hour for meditation, check out then quick lunch. I'll do yoga after I check in this afternoon. Right now I need my meditation; guess lunch will be something from the rack at the café downstairs."

Meditation enabled Alex to cleanse her mind and refresh before an event. Her years of learning high-level meditation enabled her to allow the mind to dismiss and cleanse any thoughts that came to mind during the meditation. After meditation she could finalize her noon and afternoon plans.

11:40 am

Alex was on her way for the noon hunt. She would stay away from Fulton Street until late afternoon and evening. Goetz was known to get out of the office most days. One route was to leave the casino from the Poydras street exit and walk to the bowling alley via Convention Center Boulevard, visit his lady friend then walk over to the Riverwalk and stroll through the food and shopping areas, finally exiting via the Riverwalk at their Poydras Street/Hilton exit then back to Harrah's. Alex would do the opposite route beginning at the Poydras Street/Hilton exit, have lunch at the one of the food area take-outs and take a seat in the food court area where she could watch for him.

"Ok, then let's consider completing my route with a stop at the bowling alley and Fulton Street, or else reversing the route through the Riverwalk back through the Hilton at Drago's."

"Check: change of clothes, new look; check: fresh; weapons Check: confidence is back."

Alex was on her way out the door again.

The trip was uneventful no sighting of Goetz, she did not find Goetz's lady friend at the bowling alley but it gave Alex a chance regain her total confidence.

"Ok, I'm going the Fulton Street route back to the hotel." In her mind, this morning was sufficiently suppressed for now. Alex turned left as she exited Fulton Street and headed toward her room to check out.

As she completed her walk back to the Marriott, her plans for the remainder of the day were in focus: "My stay tonight is at the French Market Inn on Decatur Street, next door to Goetz'

Pontalba apartment building."

On her way to the hotel Alex did a second review of her mental list for her next steps. "Ok, check out, leave the car at the Marriott tonight, exchange one overnight bag; pick up new bag plus a spare; check each bag for clothing, accessories, ID for this afternoon-evening plus one for tomorrow morning; double check weapons."

"Time to check in to the hotel for tonight," she thought as she completed her walk on
Decatur Street and approached the front entrance of the French Market Inn. She was especially alert since tonight's hotel was immediately next to Goetz's apartment building.

"Hi, I'm Nancy Beaudoin, I have a reservation for tonight" as she handed the French Market Inn receptionist her photo ID and credit card."

A middle-aged woman, nicely dressed with a cheerful, yet professional smile replied: "Welcome Miss Beaudoin, your room is ready. We're delighted to have you staying with us."

"Thank you, I'm looking forward to being here," she replied.

"Can we have our bellman help you with your luggage?"

"No, thank you. I have a small bag in my car."

"I don't have a record of you staying with us before. Let me review the layout of the Inn and the location of your room."

Following a few minute chart of the facility and discussion of the amenities, Alex was on her way up the stairs to her room. Once in the room it was time to get refreshed and finalize plans the rest of the day.

"First, yoga and meditation - boy do I need them both." She immediately went into her yoga routine.

An hour and ten minutes later she came out of her meditation.

"I really needed that. Ok, let's get ready for the rest of the day."

The plan: Her focus was on business. See spoke out loud and sometimes whispered as she slowly paced throughout the room:

"Cover Doubletree to Gumbo Pot, Kill Sites 1 and 4 from four o'clock through five fifteen this afternoon," she reviewed in her mind. Alex had committed each of the kill sites to memory. Kill Sites 1 and 4 from Alex's notes:

> *Kill Site 1 – Doubletree Hotel Building – overlooking the rear Canal/St.Peters Street casino entry/exit. WOW Restaurant, first floor Doubletree. Not a good or acceptable kill site. Ok for sighting Goetz' entry or exit. Not possible to take action if is sighted, plus Goetz is not known to use to use or visit the restaurant. [Staying at the Doubletree Hotel 4th night]*

> *Kill Site 4 – Gumbo Pot Restaurant outdoor fenced area overlooking Trolley stop at Toulouse Street (Jax Brewery). Route most used by Goetz to and from Harrah's/Canal Street entrance. From inside the fenced outdoor patio, good sighting spot, but impossible to get out in time to affect a close-up kill. Best to practice and consider being at the Trolley stop and Decatur Street area of Toulouse Street for Goetz's trip to work or trip from work. Practice this one a few more times.*

"Then walk to Gordon Biersch, Fulton Street for forty-five minutes; see if the lady friend leaves the bowling alley to meet

Goetz; if so, where. If not spotted, return to kill site 4, the Gumbo Pot at the Toulouse Trolley stop. Between trolley stops, walk to and from the Gumbo Pot then wait outside the Gumbo Pot restaurant fence area to see if Goetz gets off the trolley. At six thirty this evening, walk from the Gumbo Pot/Jax Brewery area to Café du Monde then back to the French Market Inn, repeat."

With her afternoon and evening plan in place, Alex was ready for the afternoon and evening. As she walked to Kill Site 1, her focus was forced on the evening as she repeated her plans in her mind.

"Kill Site 1 – best to have early evening snack at WOW with view of the one entry/exit then walk the perimeter away from the casino."

"The walk feels great, this is a great start for the evening," as she completed the walk to the first site.

Next; food at WOW restaurant - chef's salad.

Alex walked the perimeter of Kill Site 1 twice after her lunch. Uneventful.

"Ok, back to Kill Site 4. I like this one so much better. Besides, the trolley ride again," Alex said in a low voice to herself.

Once she arrived at the trolley stop and departed, she felt much better about her chances here. "This then Fulton Street later, much, much better. Just stick to my plan, stick to my plan," she reminded herself

"No action here this afternoon; it's on to Fulton Street."

Alex sat on a bench near the Ruth Chris outdoor patio inside the Fulton Street gates for the first twenty minutes of her work here. She moved to an outdoor table at Gordon Biersch where she had a great view of the area. Again, no sightings of Goetz or his lady friend.

"Alright, keep to the plan, back to Kill Site 4. Be careful, you're becoming a frequent visitor to the site and area. I just have to be successful tonight; I can feel it."

She patrolled the area as planned until the Calliope began. "Ok, time to head for Café du Monde and finish for the night."

The walk past the Café didn't find Goetz, his lady friend or his friend from last night. She walked back past the Café and up the steps to the top of Washington Square to a bench overlooking the Mississippi.

"It's a fabulous place. I hope I can still appreciate it after my kill here," she thought to herself.

She sat for another fifteen minutes, "The hunt is on hold for now." As she left the square, and walked across the intersection to go to her hotel, she decided to turn right to go to the Café Pontalba for a bite to eat. The Café was one of her designated kill sites, but tonight she just wanted to end the day with a bite to eat. She was met at the door by an anxious waiter:

"Dinner for one? Or are you meeting someone?"

Slightly startled still focusing on the present, "Oh. No. Just one. Thanks. I'm just going to have something light." Then, "Do you have a seat where I can face the Cathedral." Her instincts had kicked in so that she was seated with her back to the back of the restaurant facing the entry and the Cathedral Square.

Alex enjoyed a dish of Creole Red Beans and rice, tempted to try their crawfish etouffee. "Not tonight, tomorrow will be another full day."

Thirty minutes later she walked around the corner to her room.

"It's strange having a room next door to Goetz's apartment building. I've got to be at my best first thing tomorrow," she reminded herself.

Another thirty minutes later, exhausted from the day, Alex was ready for bed, her plans for tomorrow in place. She declared today a success.

She hoped the man from Fulton Street was alive. "Unintended consequences….unintended consequences," she muttered as she fell asleep.

During the night the story of her father's death came to her while she slept. Alex had heard the story in parts told to her by her Uncle Kent and Brother Bo. Although she wasn't there when it happened, the story had been told so many times she could relive it vividly. The dream appeared in whole to her tonight.

Uncle Kent had served seven years in the U.S. Marine Corp during which he survived three years in the Viet Nam War. After his marine duties, Kent came back to Cherokee and was instrumental in enlarging and leading the security force for the Eastern Cherokee Tribe and their ever-growing casino, hotel and tribal entertainment complex. It was Kent who hired his brother-in-law Carl as a member of Qualla Security.

Kent reminds others quietly that he remembers the death of Carl as vividly as if it was yesterday.

Kent had received a call that there was going to be a drug deal on Qualla Land that likely involved some of the Harrah's employees. It was nearly midnight. He immediately called Carl.

"Carl, I need to pick you up to check out a possible drug deal. I'll be at your place in ten minutes."

"I'll be ready. You got the guns or do I need more?"

"Bring your revolver and twelve gauge."

"Ronnie, have some back-up ready. Carl and I are going to 3-7-2, that's 3-7-2 Mark's Trail Road, that's Mark's Trail Road; suspected drug deal."

Kent picked Carl up at his house. The location of the suspected drug deal was less than ten minutes away.

"Ok, Carl, we need to be careful, don't know who these guys are. If they're inside the house we'll call back-up. They're on stand-by."

Carl checked his side gun and twelve-gauge, made sure they were fully loaded, and then loaded extra shells into his vest.

Carl asked, "Ever had anything like this at this house?"

"No. Never been there. I know the area pretty well, but never been at this house."

"Ok, we'll park here and walk. It's the third house on the right. Damn, no lights, no moon. When we get there, let's go to the front of the house and hit the ground until we hear or see something."

Two minutes later Carl whispered "Over here," as he crawled to the right side of the house.

"Kent, Kent, over here," as shots rang out.

"Carl, you ok?"

"Yeah, they're over here."

Shots were fired in Carl's direction. More shots were fired.

Kent called into dispatch whispering, "Mayday, Mayday! Officers under fire at 372 Mark's Trail. Mayday, Mayday, send back-up. It's Kent and Carl."

"Carl?"

"Yeah, I'm here, to your left."

"Stay down, I'm coming toward you."

All was quiet for a few minutes.

Then shots came from another direction.

"Abort, Carl, Abort."

Carl got up slightly from his lying position and began to crawl toward Kent.

A barrage of shots came from both directions just as the Cherokee Police back-up could be seen driving into the yard.

"Carl, these guys must have infrared. Stay flat on the ground. Stay down."

No response.

The back-up officers moved cautiously toward the directions where the shots had come from. Kent turned on his flashlight. Carl was lying on the ground.

One of the back-up officers moved back to Kent and saw Carl lying on the ground. He worked himself between Carl and Kent.

"No, No, No." Kent spoke out loudly.

"Kent, we have an ambulance on the way. Let's hope for the best."

"He's my brother-in-law, my sister's husband."

The other back-up officer stood up from kneeling and checking on Carl, "Jack, let's get Kent in the car until the ambulance gets here."

Three minutes later the ambulance arrived. The EMS declared Carl was dead.

"Pretty much my fault," said Kent as he fought off tears and got into the passenger seat of the back-up officer's car.

"We'll go back to the station and regroup. Then if you're ok with it, we'll go to his home and tell his family. I'll be with you and try to bring her minister. Do you know who that is?"

Kent gave the name of the minister and the church.

The group arrived at Carl's house at 3:50 am.

Alex has seen the scene of their arrival and visit in her mind hundreds of times.

The remainder of the day was full of friends, family, the clergy and the funeral home.

Alex woke from her dream crying. The difficult day and the vivid memory of her father's death were fresh in her mind; her earlier mistake might have cost someone else their father. Alex would never forget the day her father died and for her family it changed their destinies forever. Each one had sadness and issues to deal with for the rest of their lives.

Chapter 6

Day Three

Rules among assassins include:

- *Multitasking doesn't work. It's an assumed failure;*
- *Focus – Focus – Focus. 100% is never enough;*
- *Complex settings require the very, very best you have; and*
- *Failure isn't an option.*

August 13, 2015, 5:30 am

French Market Inn, New Orleans.

Alex awoke at her usual time and began her morning routine. Today would be another full work day, hopefully a successful one. As she prepared for her morning run her mind was on her sister Jena. Today was Jena's birthday...it would be hard not to call her but there was too much risk of being traced. It was tough too to think of having a successful kill on a family birthday. Not what you want to remember for the rest of your life. Although Jena played a major role in the financial aspects of Alex's work, she was not aware of the actual details of Alex's missions and the killings. The two sisters had agreed to this. She did believe the missions were related to tribal business.

"Ok, Alex, out the door, let's make it a great start."

Once out the door, Alex got her bearings as she walked past the front desk.

"Good morning," came a cheerful surprise from behind the front desk computer screen.

"Good morning to you," Alex responded.

"Off to a grand start of the day, are we?"

"I'm hoping it's great," replied Alex.

Today's exercise started with a half-hour run along the riverfront, down Poydras Street back two blocks past the French Market, back and forth north to south one street east at a time. As she ran her thoughts returned to Jena and not calling her on her birthday. Alex knew NSA and other agencies could track any phone call to or from anywhere; even burner phones. There is no way she could take a chance of anyone tracing her back to being in New Orleans today. Just like not stopping to see Jena on the way to or from New Orleans. Fort Walton Beach is just half hour from Interstate 10. Jena lives twenty miles from the exit.

She returned to the hotel for her final mental checklist; clothing, weapons, sites to visit, the entire morning routine, the hotel change, the new hotel. This morning she would start the day as Nancy Beaudoin until checking out of the French Market Inn hotel then convert to "Nancy Cole," her designated person for the day and check in to the Marriott on Canal Street. First, she would work the designated *"Kill Site 4."*

From her notes again:

> *Gumbo Pot Restaurant outdoor fenced patio overlooking Trolley stop at Toulouse Street (Jax Brewery). Route most used by Goetz to and from Harrah's Canal Street entrance. From inside the fenced outdoor patio area, good sighting area, but impossible to get out in time to affect a close-up kill. Best to practice and consider being at the Trolley stop*

shelter for a shot between the Trolley stop shelter for a shot at Goetz between the Trolley stop and Decatur Street area of Toulouse Street for Goetz's trip to work or from work. Practice this one a few more times.

Alex had decided to be at the site between eight o'clock and eight forty-five in the morning. Her previous visits had discovered very little street surveillance in this area so she was comfortable spending the time there being in the open. At eight forty five she would have breakfast at the open air patio area of the Gumbo Pot Restaurant. This would provide further time in case Goetz walked from his apartment to the trolley to Harrah's on the hotel side of Poydras. Then she would return to her hotel room, change into one of her other New Orleans tourist outfits before checking out of the room and consider moving the car to the next location, the Provincial Hotel.

"Parking is a bitch, maybe I'll leave it at the Marriott. I'll decide once I'm ready to move."

Kill Site 6 is the Hilton/Riverwalk second floor café and Drago's first floor restaurant.

Kill site 6 –Hilton Hotel/Riverwalk – Seating at Drago's overlooking Poydras Street and intersection. Goetz does visit the second floor café for meetings with people – near the hotel registration area. Goetz also stops for lunch and after-hour drinks at Drago's and the first floor restaurant. Good sighting site, possible kill site. Second part of the site is the Riverwalk retail area and food court. Extensive area but Goetz is known to stroll here with his lady friends.

Alex had tried this spot in front of Harrah's Hotel on her last trip; it was congested with check-ins, check-outs, valets and bellmen chasing around, but she couldn't stake it out long for fear of being watched. She would observe from the open-air café area on Fulton Street this morning then spend some time during lunch hour and after five o'clock this afternoon.

Alex put her focus back on today's work. She finished dressing and out the door to the Gumbo Pot and Kill Site 4. It was only a block away from her hotel, weather was beautiful, people were on their way to work. A few early morning tourists were milling around. Café du Monde was nearly full as were the other coffee shops.

Her post began with taking a seat at the Toulouse Street trolley shelter where she joined a handful of others, mostly tourists, seated waiting for the trolley.

"Ok, great view of the area," she thought to herself. "I'll have 30 to 40 seconds to get in line of his path when I see him."

"Great choice, this was a great choice for one of the kill sites," she thought wearing a slight smile. It validated her preparation for the mission.

8:15 am

Alex left her seat at the trolley shelter and walked to Decatur Street. "OK, stay loose." As she walked a block toward Goetz apartment; then turned and walked back to the trolley shelter.

"Ten more minutes, this is such a good site, maybe he was drunk last night and he's going to work late today. Just ten more minutes, maybe fifteen minutes. I hate to go inside the patio for breakfast and see him walk by."

"One more walk past Goetz's apartment building then over to

Café du Monde; maybe he's there meeting someone."

Alex completed her route then back to the Trolley stop.

"Time for breakfast," she said as she walked toward the Gumbo Pot entrance.

Alex entered the Gumbo Pot open air patio at nine-ten am. Still no Goetz. She spotted a small table overlooking the street. Fortunately for Alex, business was slow here. This was more of a lunch, evening and night-spot. Her table location gave her a good view of the sidewalk, Goetz was expected to walk by on his way to work. Her waiter was quick to introduce himself, took her order of yogurt with fresh fruit and a glass of apple juice. She reminded him she was not in a hurry, but the order was on her table in a few minutes.

"Crap! I need to spend thirty minutes eating two small scoops of yogurt," she thought.

During her wait, Alex fought off thinking about her sister. Jena is eight years older than Alex, and has always been a great role-model and big sister. They were both very close to their mother. While attending University of Georgia, Jena performed the Cherokee Jingle Dance at Tribal events. The highlight was Ocmulgee one of the most significant Indian Festivals in the Southeast. The dance was a highlight of the festival and Jena was a true star dancer. She had learned the dance from her aunt at Qualla when she was 7 years old. Her Aunt and friends handmade the dress and all of the bead work with thousands of beads in the foot-ware, cuffs and collar of the fabulous costumes Jena wore all of the years she performed. Now she owns her own dance studio at Fort Walton Beach.

"Ok, heads up!" She told herself. "Focus on your target." She reminded herself again, "It's likely this 80 to 100 yards of sidewalk will be one of the best spot to hit Goetz."

She reminded the waiter she was good, paid her bill. "Ok if I sit here for a few minutes?"

"Sure, are you sure I can't get you something else?" He asked.

Alex busied herself with a small note pad, "No thanks, I'm good." She continued to keep her eyes on what she hoped was Goetz' path to work.

Just as she gathered herself to leave, "Crap, there he is."

"Dammit, I can't get out to him."

"So there he is, dressed his best; cell phone to his ear. No briefcase. He had the look on his face as though he had just won five million dollars...or stole five million dollars. Dammit, I could have hit him just now."

"Okay, set this as the spot for this afternoon for his trip back to his apartment." Alex watched helplessly standing inside the fenced in patio as Goetz boarded the trolley and was on his way to the casino.

"I knew this was a great site. This and Fulton Street."

"I'll get out of here, walk the sidewalk back toward his apartment then rehearse it again after checking out of the French Market Inn." Alex spent the next five to seven minutes walking the stretch of sidewalk then pacing for a few minutes as though she was waiting for a ride. She stopped at a park bench first to see if anyone was following her. She had spent too much time in the area this morning. She would study this again when she checked into her room at the Provincial.

"If I don't hit him this afternoon or evening, this might be my best site for tomorrow morning."

On her walk back to the French Market Inn to check out, Alex knew now that she would succeed.

"I knew my preparation was good, I just knew it. I just need to keep focused on my plans; and one piece of good timing."

"I'm leaving the car at the Marriott parking garage, I'll check it out after checking out of the French market Inn, then leave the overnight bag in the car. I have my bag with the morning outfit and Nancy Cole ID. OK. That's the plan." She took time to check out of her room and change to Nancy Cole.

"I have three hours before checking in to the new hotel. My gut tells me that my best plan is to go back to Fulton Street then over to the Hilton and Riverwalk. It's the best use of the time plus the food court is there."

The tour was uneventful, but she was more comfortable with each place as a kill site. Leaving the Riverwalk, she walked to the Marriott parking garage to pick up her overnight bag for her check-in at the Hotel Provincial.

Once in the room at the Hotel Provincial, Alex sat in her meditation pose. She felt a need to focus on her mission this afternoon and evening.

"Ok, yoga first, then meditation then change of clothes."

Coming out of her meditation, Alex was refreshed with new energy for the second half of the day's mission. The hour and fifteen minute routine had proven to give her great new energy for the second half of the day.

"Check, weapons. Check, clothing for this afternoon and evening. Check, Kill Site 4. Check, walk between the Washington Square and the Toulouse trolley station. Take the three pre-planned routes. Walk fast from the trolley stop shelter and the square. Walk slowly from the square back to the trolley stop. Begin at four forty-five this afternoon. Do not go into the Gumbo Pot." She repeated under her breath to herself three times. It was a near duplicate of this morning.

"I'll think of Jena after work is done."

On her walk from the new hotel to her planned post, Alex whispered to herself as her eyes followed the streets and people, "One of the good parts around this area is it's easy to get lost in the crowd."

She continued her walk around Jackson Square then through the center of the square. Then she spent time walking the intersection at the Cathedral and the Café Pontalba across the intersection.

"The artists and tourists here won't care to look at me or remember me. Besides, it's very entertaining to see it all."

She walked up to the door of the Café but hesitated to go inside. There were only a handful of people there and the staff might be able to remember something about me if ever questioned.

"Unlikely, but don't take a chance," she reminded herself.

Her constant internal chatter kept her focused on the mission that had started this evening at Washington Square and a quick look at Café du Monde.

"No Goetz or the other guy."

She followed her plan of a slow walk from Washington Square to the Gumbo Pot, Toulouse Street trolley stop then waited for ten minutes at the trolley stop.

"Ok, back to Washington Square then wait there for ten minutes," she said to herself.

She cautiously repeated this routine until seven thirty with no sightings.

"I've got to get out of here. Way too much exposure to locals and cameras," as she walked from Washington Square to the Cathedral, Pontalba Restaurant intersection.

"Lots of activity here. Plenty of cover. Let's stay for a half-hour and see if Goetz shows up here."

An hour later Alex moved to a table inside Cafe du Monde.

8:10 pm

Alex called it a day, "Nothing here."

As she walked to her hotel plans for tomorrow were clear. "It's back to Fulton Street and the Riverwalk. No Gumbo Pot. I think I've worn out Kill Site 4. I've been there more than most of the people who live and work there. There's been enough time since the problem on Fulton Street. I'm comfortable that I won't be recognized; my fear is gone, plus it's a very fertile site. I can go from there then do the Riverwalk and the Hilton, have lunch at Dragos then check in to my night at the Doubletree.

Plans for tomorrow were imbedded by the time she reached her room.

As she sat in the easy chair in the room and snacked on Cliff Bars and fruit, her thoughts turned to Jena. It was her birthday.

"Holy crap! It's her fortieth, this is the big one! It's her birthday and I can't call her."

Jena and Alex have always been close. She is the perfect big sister; eight years older than Alex; Mom's helper from the time Alex was born; an incredible role-model for Alex during her youth and teens. Mom's helper and big sister to Bo and Alex when their father was killed. Jena was a dancer for the Tribe from age seven and one of the first to perform at major festivals In Cherokee and at Okmulgee. She represented the Eastern Band of Cherokee throughout her middle school and high school years, performed in the Cherokee presentation "Unto These Hills" during her high school years and continued representing the Eastern Band of Cherokee throughout her college years at festivals and events throughout the southeastern and mid-Atlantic states.

Jena's work and talent has paid off. She is the sole owner of her dance studio in Fort Walton Beach, Florida and continues to participate in Indian gatherings. She and her husband, Jordan, have three children. Jordan manages three Applebee restaurants for a private owner. He is unaware of any of the activities of Alex and any relationship of these activities with his wife.

Jordan is the son of a full blood Choctaw mother and a one-fourth blood Cherokee father. His father is the son of a former Cherokee farmer and white head-of-household. His ancestors did not leave Georgia during the removal years. The stories they carried forward for their family and descendants were first-hand accounts of the brutality of the government.

Jena and Jordan met while attending University of North

Carolina. Jordan was a member of the track and field team as a long-distance runner. Jena was well known throughout the campus as a dancer. Jena and Jordan met during their third year of college at a University Cherokee festival attended by hundreds Native American students. Following that meeting, they became followers of each other's talents and performances; Jordan with Jena's dancing; Jena with Jordan's running as a member of the UNC track and field team plus his non-University 26-mile marathon competitions.

Jordan joined the United States Air Force immediately following graduation. He was assigned a junior officers' role at Eglin Air Force Base in the panhandle of Florida following his graduation from the Air Force Academy.

Jena and Jordan continued their relationship when it was possible for them to meet. They were married two years later at Qualla Boundary in Cherokee. Following their marriage they moved to a home near the Air Force base in Fort-Walton Beach, Florida where Jena taught dance at a private studio. Jordan left the Air Force after completing his six years of duty and joined a management team at a large restaurant chain based in Pensacola. Jena opened her own dance studio in Fort Walton Beach three years later.

Alex reminded herself, "Mom and Bo will call her, even Uncle Kent might call her. She knows that I can't call when I'm on a mission. I'll call her first thing when I pick up my car."

"Ok, I need to be ready for tomorrow. I like my plan." She said out loud as she walked herself through the plan for tomorrow.

"The first kill site at Fulton Alley, move the car, a full tour of the Riverwalk, lunch at Drago's at the Hilton."

"Weapons, Ok; clothes, Ok; I'm ready. Tomorrow will be a great day."

"Jena and Jordan are probably having a great night out at a great restaurant." Alex had a nice smile, took a deep breath and released the day.

Fifteen minutes later Alex was ready for bed; her mind was focused on the next day. Today had been another exhausting one, but days on a mission always are.

Twenty minutes later she was asleep.

Chapter 7

Day Four

"There are those who say the kill doesn't matter. They are fools and liars. I can laugh at misses, pass up an easy shot when there is a reason, and come home skunked but happy. All of that doesn't matter. The kill matters and the manner of the kill matters." Robert Elma

August 14, 2015, 5:30 am

Alex woke at her usual time performed her morning mental and physical routines. Her senses were at their peak; "Today will be the day" she said to herself. She had put the past two days behind her.

Her morning run today was south of the Washington Square along the river then back north to the Riverwalk, down the Riverwalk area then return to her the Hotel Provincial .

As she ran she whispered her morning plans twice: "Step one today, to Fulton Street then over to the Marriott parking garage for my next change, back to the hotel for shower and check-out. Ok, that's in place. Back to the Marriott parking garage to drop off both bags, then on to the Riverwalk and Drago's."

Alex showered and changed then out the door to the Marriott 4th floor parking garage. She wore a light cotton top and shorts, no brand markings, gray-blue. Today it was forecast to be a high of 93 degrees with some humidity. Once at the car her instincts took over. She began checking the car: Tires were good; parking exit ticket was in place in the glove box along with more-than-enough cash; no dents or scratches. "She's ready to roll," she said.

"Now to Fulton Street. I'll walk the area from the front gate past the bowling alley and return."

On her entry she spotted a woman who looked like it could be Goetz's lady friend walking about twenty feet ahead of her.

"That's her, even from the back I can tell, that's the lady."

"Ok, keep a safe distance behind her, be sure she enters the bowling alley then reverse the route and look for Goetz coming toward me. This time I won't miss."

The lady did enter the bowling alley.

"Reverse, walk at a normal pace, and focus on the front gate area for Goetz coming my way." Alex's heart was about to beat out of her chest.

She stopped for a deep breath, "calm down, calm down, Cowart, you're not new at this. Just follow your gut. Do it, just do it right."

She reached for her weapon. "Ok, that's ready."

Half hour later, still no sign of Goetz.

"Let's get out of here; we've been here too long."

"Back to the parking garage, then to the hotel for check-out."

Per her plan, it was time to check out of the Hotel Provincial and get the rest of the day underway. A different lady was at the front desk, although she looked much the same as the nice lady yesterday.

"I do hope your stay was good, Ms. Cole. We're sorry you're not staying with us longer, and we do hope you will stay with us again."

Alex returned the comments with, "Yes, thank you, it was very nice. I think I will stay longer the next time."

Her next move was to drop her overnight bag at the car. From there she continued on her route to the Riverwalk and Hilton. On her way she re-routed herself back to Fulton Street where she walked from the entrance to a block past the bowling alley. She then continued to the Riverwalk, entering at the food court side of the Riverwalk as she had planned. Her walk through the length of the mall ended at the Hilton Hotel escalator.

"Time for a break."

11:27 am

Early lunch. She made her way to the bistro tables of Drago's in the Hilton Hotel convention center. It was hot outside; she needed to pace herself for any outdoor work this afternoon. She ordered iced tea reminding the waitress, "I'm not in a hurry, take your time." Alex had chosen a bistro table facing Poydras with a view of the Poydras entrance of the Harrah's Casino across the large intersection. The seat also gave her a view of the Hilton Convention Center Poydras street entrance. Following lunch Alex had planned to spend some time here then stroll the area between the Hilton and Harrah's Hotel to spot Goetz.

Ten minutes later, "Holy Crap! There he is." She spotted Goetz walking hurriedly across the intersection toward the Hilton.

"There's something different going on" she said to herself. "He's carrying a briefcase, he never carries a briefcase. Dammit, he's coming into the Hilton entrance." She put three dollars on the table, nodded to the waiter and waited at the door to see where he was going once he entered the Hotel and conference complex.

She watched as Goetz entered the Hilton Convention Center doorway; Alex exited Drago's and caught up with Goetz.

"What's with the briefcase? Where's he going?"

He turned left up the escalator toward the hotel registration area. She held back and followed staying a disciplined twenty feet behind. Goetz walked past the registration desk, then to the second escalator to the next level and headed toward the train and trolley overpass to the hotel room lobby area. Goetz turned right into the entry and hallway into the Building 3 hotel rooms, she followed. As he headed down the hallway he suddenly turned left and disappeared. Alex stopped, caught her breath.

"Be careful Alex," she whispered to herself. Now she moved slowly.

To her surprise, Goetz had walked onto an open courtyard overlooking the Mississippi. A plaque on the wall read 'Mark Twain Courtyard'. At the end of the courtyard there were three benches facing the river. She watched Goetz seat himself next to another man. As Goetz reached the bench, the other man stood up to shake his hand.

"It's the man I saw him with at Café du Monde Tuesday evening." "Ok," she thought to herself, "Let's hit him on his return." Going out into the courtyard wasn't an option, cameras, it was wide open. She couldn't stay in the corridor waiting for him to come out.

Alex walked down the corridor the way she came in, "Let's get ready for this." She walked back through the hallway to a large open lobby area. "This is it; he'll probably come back the same way he came in."

As she surveyed the lobby area to see what might be her best plan, "I need a place where I can see him coming down the hallway, then go from there."

"Ok, I'll sit at the flower/plant box leading to the stairway/escalators to the lower level Riverwalk retail store area."

As she sat on the wooden trim of the flower/plant box, "Perfect. I can see all the way down the hallway."

"Ok, when I spot him, my best shot is to meet him walking over the train-trolley overpass. Lobby here is too wide open. I can't chase him, I need to meet him."

Alex walked across the lobby area from her sitting site to the overpass then crossed the overpass. "Excellent, I've got enough time to cross the overpass and walk toward him when I see him exit the Building 3 entryway. Excellent, that's it," she whispered to herself.

There was enough walking traffic, everyone seemed focused on their destination within the hotel. She began her wait by sitting at the plant-flower box.

She repeated her plan to herself; "When I see Goetz round the corner from the corridor I'll walk toward him, need to stay on his left side, stay on his left, he'll have the briefcase in his right hand."

"Ok, get the weapon ready, stay on his left side and deliver the dose." "Aim for the mouth and upper lip."

Alex tried to look casual and busy, like she belonged at this spot at this time. Six minutes later Goetz exited the Mark Twain Courtyard and headed down the building 3 hallway. The other man was walking at least ten feet behind him.

"The other guy has the briefcase!" she noted to herself.

Alex focused on her moves as she left her site. "Across the lobby, cross the train-trolley overpass, reverse at the end of the overpass; stay on the left, weapon ready."

Just as she reached the end of the overpass and reversed her course, she saw Goetz exit the Building 3 hallway.

"Ok, I've got him," she thought. She reached for her weapon with her left hand, focused on having her weapon comfortably in place, walked toward her target. The instant it was in place she took a deep breath put her eagle-eye focus on Goetz and walked at a brisk-but-steady pace along with the others walking across the overpass.

"Now: Four-three-two-one." With a forceful blow into the reed she expelled the deadly load of poison. "Perfect."

"Keep walking, don't look back," she said to herself.

"Not so fast, just keep"....then she spotted the mystery man at the small gift shop and convenience shop in the lobby area near the exit to the Riverwalk. Alex couldn't stop, and turned toward a meeting room where she could observe the lobby area and the mystery man. He paid the cashier, picked up his briefcase heading toward the down escalator for the Riverwalk. She headed for him but stayed a safe distance. "Who is this guy?" The mystery man took a sharp left at the end of the escalator ride and headed out the door toward the entry door to Drago's. He headed toward a courtesy SUV with 'The Fairgrounds Racetrack and Casino' sign on its side. He got into the vehicle and left.

Alex suddenly realized what all had just happened. Her heart was beating so hard she could hear it. "Ok, focus, focus, and regroup. Get to the car," she said to herself. She headed toward the Marriott parking garage in as casual a pace as was possible.

"Goetz," she said to herself, "I don't hear any ambulance, police. It must have worked," she reminded herself. "It was a perfect shot. I'll get a message in a few hours" she assured herself.

"Hey, wait" she thought, Goetz didn't have the briefcase, the other guy had it." "Who is this guy? "Something's going on here."

Now the sound of sirens wailed through the air.

When she arrived at the car in the Marriott parking garage, she put everything she had into the back seat, got in, buckled her seatbelt, turned the air conditioning to high. Alex checked to be sure the Carol Shea driver's license and other identification was in the car's glove box where she had left it after arriving the first day.

Alex wasn't familiar with the Fairground Racetrack and Casino. It had not been part of her research and planning for this mission. She needed to find it and see it firsthand. She followed her car's GPS/Google map, studied it with her paper maps to route her trip, avoiding street cameras wherever possible. She would avoid entering the casino area and racetrack too due to high levels of security cameras.

"This works" she said to herself; "It's four or five blocks from an I-10 East entrance. I'll settle for a drive by. I've got homework to do."

An hour later from within the Fairgrounds facility, the mystery man tried to reach Goetz by a coded text message. No response. He had work to do the remainder of the afternoon. He was unaware of what had happened to Goetz.

As the mystery man was packing his personal briefcase to leave for the day the Chief Security Officer at the Fairgrounds complex asked if he had heard anything about the executive or manager from Harrah's being dead. The mystery man stopped. Every muscle and bone in his body froze.

"What? What did you say?"

The Chief answered, "I didn't mean to startle you. I just wondered if you had heard that one of the guys who ran Harrah's was dead. I think the Assistant Manager".

"No... No, but call me if you hear anything."

The mystery man picked up the 'Goetz' briefcase after the security chief left the office area. "What the hell do I do with this thing?" he said to himself. "Just get it out of here, I'll put it in my trunk, just get it out of here" he said in a whisper to himself.

Michael McFarlane had been Chief Security Officer at the Fairgrounds for seven years and was well connected to the police and the other casino security officers in the New Orleans area.

The mystery man got in his car to travel home. He tried one more time to reach Goetz. No reply. He drove to his home in Slidell in silence, his mind in a whir. His whole existence could be in jeopardy. "If it is Goetz, how did he die, did someone kill him or did he have a heart attack."

The mystery man's mind couldn't stop. He made a turn into a shopping center parking area to catch his breath. "I've got to get a grip so my wife doesn't see me like this," he said out loud. He got out of his car and walked around it twice. "I'd better go into the shopping center instead of being out here. People will think I'm crazy." Following a five minute walk around inside the shopping center and dozens of deep breaths, he shook it off, got back into his car and continued his drive home.

The potion delivered to Goetz stunned him and immobilized him in a few seconds. He dropped some papers from his hands. He struggled to bring his arms up to his chest, neck and face. Two men stopped, one yelled out "Heart attack, the man is having a heart attack." Goetz's arms and legs flailed uncontrollably; his lungs had been paralyzed. He was dead within ninety seconds. Hilton security guards scrambled to call an EMS team and ambulance. Police were not called.

An autopsy the next day would record the cause of death as "unknown."

When the man who had met Goetz arrived home, he tried to act as any other day. Dinner would be ready in 45-minutes and he usually went to the office at his home. The first thing he did was turn on the local news, sat in his desk chair and stared at the TV. He was afraid to try to reach Goetz by phone or text. If he is dead, if there is something going on, I don't want to have anyone see my phone number on his phone. "I worried a few times about Goetz. I don't know why, but I did," he said out loud to himself.

Chapter 8

When the Adrenalin Runs Out

"The best kind of friend is the kind you can sit on the porch with, never say a word, and then walk away feeling like it was the best conversation you've ever had."

August 14, 2015, 3:45 pm

Alex received a coded text message on her burner phone two hours and thirty minutes after leaving New Orleans: "Success – OK at compound." She mentally calculated that she was about an hour and a half from Holley.

It was good news since she was feeling the let-down and exhaustion coming. The adrenalin rush from the past four days was beginning to wane. The additional four and one-half hours from the Holley compound to her Jacksonville home was not possible this evening. She welcomed the stop and car exchange, but sorely needed a private and secure place to crash.

Her thoughts turned from the events of earlier in the day, the killing, the discovery of a potential Goetz partner, to the thought of someone identifying her while she was in New Orleans. This always enters the mind of an assassin.

The thought ran through her mind: "If Goetz saw me it's ok, he's dead; no way he would have been able to describe me before he died; there was no sign he recognized me at the time I killed him. If the others saw me at the Fulton Street site they most likely won't remember what or who the saw. If street cameras caught me, it's still unlikely they can identify me or determine what happened."

"Just get me to my car, my other clothes, my Galaxy 5 phone, my cds," she whispered to herself. She then repeated it out loud as she tightened her grip on the steering wheel and sat up straight in the car seat.

During the planning for the mission, Alex had been advised that she was welcome to stay at the Tribal Compound and leave the next day for Jacksonville if the timing of her return trip needed it. It was part of the plan she welcomed at this point.

She continued her travel east on Interstate 10 in silence.

An hour and forty minutes after the receiving the "Success – OK at compound" message, Alex arrived at the Holley site. Once she entered the driveway to the compound area she saw three people seated on the porch of the Council House. One of the three, an elderly woman, walked from the porch and met Alex as her car stopped.

"You must be our guest?" she said.

"Yes, I am."

"Oh, please come to the porch with us. Chairwoman Reed will be here in a few minutes. Please sit with us while she is on her way."

Alex welcomed the invitation.

A second woman spoke, "We're here to help you with dinner and your safety tonight."

"Thank you so much," Alex replied. "I am tired, it was a long day," she admitted. "You are all so kind."

In a few minutes a car entered the compound and drove up to the Council House. It was Tribal Chairwoman Reid. She held her arms open as she approached Alex.

"Welcome back, dear. I'm so excited to see you again. Come, see your accommodations," as she motioned for Alex to follow her. Two of the other women followed. The third stayed seated on the porch.

Chairwoman Reed spoke to Alex and the other two, "We know we won't discuss your being here or your travels. We are here to help and pleased to do so. These people will help you with anything you need; they'll provide dinner and help you with your room." The two women nodded in agreement.

Alex quietly said, "Thank you so much."

On her way to the door, Chairwoman Reed said, "Mark will be here tomorrow morning to take care of the car exchange. Someone will guard the car out front until we complete the exchange. Ladies, please help our guest get the things she'll need from the car for tonight. Mark will be here shortly to guard it."

With that, Chairwoman Reed returned to her car and drove away.

One of the ladies escorted Alex into the room where she would stay for the night. She was introduced to the other elderly lady who would be available to help her with any needs and provide Alex with dinner.

Dinner was served in silence in a private area attached to the

Council House. Alex dined alone. The dinner included an incredible fillet of fish, corn and potato along with a glass of chardonnay. Following dinner alone in a private guest room area of the Council House, Alex gathered her clothing and items from the car for the evening, showered and in a few minutes collapsed into a deep sleep. She was safe, her mission completed. Alex was unaware that the Tribal Chairwoman had returned and sat on the porch outside the Council House for nearly two hours. She was replaced by two other tribal members whose responsibility was to protect and watch over Alex. They and their replacements would serve serving three hour shifts throughout the night until Alex left the next day.

During the deep sleep of the night, Alex dreamed of the story told by her mother two weeks ago of the preparation for their niece Phyllis's jingle dance at Okmulgee in September.

On an August evening, the three sisters anxiously awaited their daughter and niece, Phyllis and an elder who would guide their work. Today was the second fitting of the new dress for the dance at Okmulgee, an intertribal regional event in September, six weeks away. It was a great honor to be chosen to perform the jingle dance. The honor was to Phyllis and all of her family. Her mother and aunts would prepare the entire costume. Their preparation included hand making the entire dress and accessories for their 19-year-old star. They will make two dresses, shoe-stockings, cuffs, head piece and hair piece, earrings, neck collar and necklace. A Qualla resident-elder would be their guide through the project.

Ocmulgee is the largest Native American gathering in the Southeastern United States. Phillis would be one of the most important individuals out of 200 performers, craftsmen, dancers and storytellers participating in the two-day event. Last year over 16,000 people came to the monument grounds to see and celebrate the event.

Phyllis had performed the jingle dance at ceremonies since she was twelve. Her teacher, and favorite aunt, was Alex's sister Jena, a well-known ceremonial dancer who now owned a dance studio in Pensacola, Florida.

Phyllis's mother, Nora, was the youngest of the three sisters; Irene, the oldest, was mother of Alex, Jena, and Bo. The middle sister, Lola, was the best seamstress and, along with their elder guide, would ensure beautiful and highest quality work. The dress was complex in style plus it had to support over 70 hanging light-weight bells; the bead work on the accessories were made of over 200,000 beads hand sewn to cloth, leather and suede. Their pattern and color scheme would include over 76,000 sky blue beads, 76,000 black beads, 36,000 white beads and 12,000 red beads. This dress was black, a second one would be made next month from sky-blue cloth and a duplicate set of accessories.

Phyllis arrived followed by the elder lady whose English name was Mattie. Mattie was escorted by two of her grandsons who immediately left the house. They would return to take Mattie back to her home. Phyllis was beaming. So were her mother and aunts, Irene and Lola. She bowed from the knees then hugged Mattie, then hugged the others. This had to be one of the best days of her young life.

Nora was hosting today's gathering. The sisters and their elder guide would complete the work of the dress fitting then the four would remain to focus on the accessories. Phyllis was not to participate in any of the work but would help with the final preparation and serving of food for the group. During the work the elder guide told stories of costumes she helped make for other dancers and the stage players actors and actresses of the famous Cherokee story "Unto These Hills."

Throughout the evening the elder guide Mattie and the three sisters entertained each other with stories about great events among the Cherokee people and how great their lives were since the tragedy of the removal from their great Cherokee Nation in

Georgia. Phyllis didn't miss a story or word.

The food consisted of traditional breads and fruit spread, hazel nuts, and an incredible mixed-fresh berry pie Nora had made that morning. Three types of herbal teas accompanied the food.

As soon as the group completed their work and disbursed, Phyllis called her Aunt Jena to thank her and tell her how great the evening was.

Chapter 9

Home

---

*"Coming home from very lonely places, all of us go a little mad:
whether from great personal success or just an all-night drive, we
are the sole survivors of a world no one has ever seen."*
                                        -John LeClarre

August 15, 2015, 5:30 am

Alex woke abruptly this morning. It took a few minutes to realize
where she was. She dressed in her yoga outfit then opened the
door to find the same elderly lady greeting her.

"Good morning, dear. What can we prepare you for breakfast?
Would you like coffee?"

"Oh, no thanks, not right now. I usually do some stretching and
exercise for forty-five minutes. Is it ok to do that?"

   The lady looked at Alex strangely and replied, "yes, certainly it
is."

"I'll need to do my exercise in the bedroom if that's ok."

"Ok, then I'll have coffee waiting for you."

"That sounds great," as she slowly closed the door.

   Alex finished her yoga routine then walked out of the room.

"I'll need my car. My fresh clothes are in it."

   The lady nodded in agreement and quickly went to the door.

In a few minutes Alex was escorted to the front porch area. Alex retrieved her clothing bag for the day from her own car and returned for her shower and breakfast.

Breakfast was just as requested, yogurt and fresh fruit...and coffee.

7:20 am

As Alex prepared to leave, two men were waiting at her car. Mark, the man who she had met when the initial car exchange took place and another man she had not met. The two men watched as Alex moved all of her belongings from the Council House room and the exchange car to hers. Alex took time to check her car inside and outside. Her phone, registration, all front and rear lights and turn signals were fine. The final check was her purse and her personal identification, including her driver's license, insurance and other identification; all of the other identification items for the four other pseudonyms were placed in a bottom compartment of her purse.

"Thank you so much, Mark, and you too Sir."

Mark spoke, "It's good to see you again. We are honored to have been here for you. We are told by Tribal Chairwoman Reed that your journey was very important to us. We are all one people. We pray the Creator grants you a long life."

Alex, holding back a tear, replied "Thank you. I am honored to be able to be a part of you and serve our cause."

As she traveled toward Interstate 10 she began to mentally move to her other life. She knew she would be free of any contact regarding the next mission for at least thirty days.

She was dressed in her favorite yoga outfit along with her best running shoes. There was a different move in her step as she fastened her seatbelt, grabbed the steering wheel and waved to Mark and the other man.

"I really do like both of my lives," she said out loud. "I really do," as she drove onto the road heading for I-10.

A few minutes later she looked around her car and began getting in the mood for the trip home.

The first music she played was *"Call Me The Breeze"*:

"Call me the breeze

I keep blowin' down the road

Well now they call me the breeze

I keepblowin'down the road

I ain't got me nobody

I don't carry me no load."

8:35 am

Alex passed the I-10 exit to Fort Walton Beach. Now it was safe to call Jena. If anyone questioned her travel today, she could claim she had been at her sister's house. The current location made it safe to activate her phone and call.

"Hi Big Sis, happy fortieth!" Alex said with an excited smile.

"Where are you, are you ok?" asked Jena.

"I'm great, just on my way home."

"Just wish I could see you; I know you have been busy and out-of-town."

"So, Big Sis, did you have a good birthday?"

"It was great. Hey, I know you're traveling. Call me when you get home; we can talk much more. Jason and the kids are great, Mom has called a few times. Oh, I'm so glad you're ok and on your way home. Love ya!"

"Love you too Sis. I'll call you when I get home."

Jena took a deep breath, "Thank Heavens she's ok."

Alex turned her music back on, smiled to herself and settled in for the remainder of the trip home.

8:48 am

Alex turned her music back on, smiled to herself and continued on I-10 east.

Her phone rang, it was Bo. "Hey Big Bo, what's up?"

"Hi Sis, what's up with you?"

"I'm traveling home."

"Don't use your cell phone when you're driving. Real quickly, Uncle Kent invited us for another fishing trip, you up for that?"

"Wow, yes. I'll call you when I get home later today."

"The trip should be in the next three or four weeks. Think about

84

it."

"I'm so excited. I love Uncle Kent's fishing trips. I'm starving for fresh fish, especially Uncle Kent's."

Bo agreed.

"Call you later when I get home. Thanks, Bo. Love ya."

"Love you too sis. Talk to you later."

The call immediately reminded her of their last trip to Uncle Kent's. "Wow," she said out loud, "What incredible news. I love Uncle Kent's house on the river, fishing with a first class bass fisherman, eating the best cooked fish ever, and Uncle Kent and his dog Chester."

"Oops, I forgot. Yoga on the riverbank."

Kent and Chester live in a St. Johns Riverfront house in Welaka, FL. Kent's love of bass fishing introduced him to the Welaka area four or five years ago. He had participated in fishing

Tournaments in Welaka, and when it was time for a major life-change he had considered the area and found his dream home on the river. The house sits on a twenty-five foot bluff with a full view of the river and the Ocala National Forest across the river on the west bank.

Alex's thoughts drifted deeper into her memory of the last visit there with Bo. I remember sitting on the deck of his riverfront house the first time we were there. It is so nice, so beautiful, and so quiet.

Uncle Kent pointed out to me, "Nothing but gators, creatures, osprey and trees...and bass."

Last time we were there Kent prepared French potato salad, fresh pole beans, corn-on-the-cob, and fresh fish Bo called catch-of-the-afternoon. I think I'll never forget it.

Kent had become a great cook since his wife had been killed in an accident. He loves to prepare meals for his guests. His green house and herb gardens include nearly thirty herbs, half of which were grown from wild North Carolina plants. He has learned which ones are best to enhance the taste of nearly any fish, especially river bass.

I suppose we'll do the same as last trip, Bo drove from Charlotte and stayed at my place in Jacksonville. The next day we arrived at Uncle Kent's around eleven o'clock, time for lunch then afternoon fishing. Chester always leads the greeting with his ear-piercing 'bo-woo' as only Chester can do. I remember Uncle Kent telling us he had learned his greeting bark from a beagle friend when he was a puppy. He was running in circles around me and Bo when we came in the door.

Uncle Kent was almost as excited as Chester, "Come on in, let's get this show on the road," with hugs all around. I guess it's hard to tell which of the four of us was most excited. The three of us and Chester bouncing from one of us to the other worked our way to the second floor deck. What a view! I remember thinking how lucky I was to be there.

Uncle Kent pointed to his pontoon boat, "Here's the boat we'll use today. Equipment and bait are already in the boat. She's ready to go."

"Ok, sis, let's get our stuff out of the car. Looks like Uncle Kent is serious about fishing."

"Lunch first, then let our lunch settle, then we'll fish," Kent advised us.

Bo said to me, just loud enough for Kent to hear," Uncle Kent says he's never been skunked while fishing. I'll bet he has a half-dozen bass already caught, hooked by a string in some spot on the river. We'd better watch him."

Uncle Kent reminded me, "Alex, you've got your own suite downstairs."

"I call it my riverbank yoga pad. I'm getting more and more excited."

In a few minutes I was heading to the first floor suite with my duffle bag and cd player, put them in the first floor room, then headed back up the stairway to the second floor for lunch.

Kent invited us to lunch with a great smile on his face, "We've got Alex's favorites, peppermint water, lemon water, fresh veggies from the County Line, a few herbs from the garden, then there's tuna salad and bread for a sandwich or on lettuce. Dig in."

I think I was just grinning; enjoying the atmosphere and the company, and the food was incredible. It feels like I'm still there, and I can't wait to go back.

Uncle Kent reminded us again, "The pontoon boat is ready to go, all the bait, lures and poles we need. How about we take off in thirty minutes; time for lunch to settle."

Bo and I agreed. Chester just kept going from person to person, excited to be part of the group.

Alex broke from her daydream and thought to herself: "The call from Bo just now and the great memories and thoughts of Uncle Kent and Welaka are just what I needed. This I-10 route returning from my mission seems like it is a thousand miles long. Looking at the mile marker, I still have a ways to go before I'm home."

In a few minutes her memories of the trip flooded back.

I can still feel the moment the boat left the dock and headed south along the west bank of the river, and seeing the incredible wilderness of the forest. I remember too Uncle Kent pointing out a half-dozen Osprey nests and Osprey along with numerous sighting of fish jumping out of the water. In twenty minutes, Kent shut the engines down to a slow crawl.

"Ok," he said, "Time to get the lines in the water. Let's see who gets the first one."

Bass fishing requires continuous casting of the lures just below the surface. Uncle Kent is an artist, Bo is pretty good. I was clumsy, but improving rapidly.

Bo had the first strike.

"Damn, that's a good sized one, Bo, keep haulin' it in," coached Kent. "Get him in close and I'll get the net."

I just stared and smiled. "This is so incredible. Go Bo!"

Not long after a bass grabbed my bait, I remember yelling out, "Hey, I think I've got one." I remember looking at my reel then the pole then the fish being drawn toward the boat. "Just keep it steady, Sis," coached Bo. Kent echoed the message. Bo grabbed the net, "Ok, sis, I've got the net, just keep reeling it in."

Once the fish was in the boat I was giddy with excitement. "Bet mine is bigger than yours, Bo."

As Bo was removing the hook from the fish, he responded "Gee,

I can't tell which one is which."

I know mine was bigger.

The trip ended with seven catches. Three were too small and were released.

"Let's head home for dinner," Uncle Kent said as the boat gained speed and headed north.

Chester headed for the bow of the boat for the ride home.

Bo spoke out over the sound of the boat engine reminding Uncle Kent and me that he had "outfished" us, saying "Keepers, Bo two, you others, one each."

"Tomorrow is another day," Kent reminded him with a smile.

Bo cleaned the fish, Kent prepared two with stuffing. I was assigned to clean and prepare the green beans and corn-on-the-cob under close guidance from my uncle.

"Let's give the fish forty-five minutes," instructed Kent. "I'll open the chardonnay." I was instructed to get the wine glasses from the first cupboard.

"Cheers, here is to a good day on the water," toasted Kent. We touched glasses, and then each of us sat back in our chair on the deck overlooking the St. Johns. Chester sat alongside me.

"I've got to be one of the luckiest women in the world," I said out loud. "Cheers!" yelled out the two men as they raised their glasses.

Forty-five minutes later and half-way through the second bottle of chardonnay, dinner was served. I switched to peppermint water after my one glass of wine. The other two didn't.

89

"Wow, this meal is incredible," Bo remarked. I totally agreed. Kent had prepared two distinctly different types of stuffing for the baked bass along with the fresh pole beans and corn, and a French potato salad.

I remember saying, "Uncle Kent, you need to open a restaurant." Bo nodded in agreement.

"No way, take the fun out of it," he replied smiling.

Dinner ended with the traditional drawing of the straws to see who would clean the kitchen and do the dishes. Bo and Kent headed out the door to the deck leaving me with the short straw in hand. Kent and Bo then turned around and helped me clean the table and rinse dishes. Chester stayed with me while I finished my chores. The two men headed back to the deck with the chardonnay. I know there's a trick or conspiracy with the drawing of the straws. I smiled and smiled.

"What an incredible day."

After a half-hour plus of story-telling, I headed for my room with a hug from each and a nose rub for Chester. Bo and Kent were still in their glory.

"One more glass," Kent said as he worked the cork out of the third bottle. Bo didn't disagree.

I remember shaking my head wondering how good they would feel the next day

"It was an incredible day," she reminded herself as she shook her head, snapping herself out of her daydream as she continued east on I-10.

9:22 am

"Ok, I should be home in two and a half hours; call Mom, call Bo, call Jena, go to the fitness room."

"Bo's call is just what I needed right now. Killing Goetz was a successful mission, but I'm glad it's over."

She drove in silence and avoided meaningful thoughts for several minutes.

The silence broke when she said out loud: "I can't keep the thoughts of the fishing trip off my mind. Guess I'm just excited about the next trip."

She drifted back to the second and third mornings of the last fishing trip.

"Yoga on the riverbank," she said out loud. My friends in Jacksonville still don't believe me.

The setting is remarkable, facing out over the river, watching all the birds, large and small without interference of humans. About forty minutes into my yoga routine, Bo yelled out, "Let's go Sis, breakfast." I couldn't believe he and Uncle Kent were awake, let alone preparing breakfast. Uncle Kent had outdone himself again; fresh raspberries and strawberries with greek yogurt and local honey.

"What is this, a royal spa?" I asked. "You live an incredible life and eat like a yoga instructor." Bo agreed, but I think he preferred a pile of scrambled eggs and hash browns.

We left the dock at eight o'clock that morning eager for a great day. The two 'choir boys' seemed sober, but I still wonder how that could be. Our fishing for two and a half hours in the morning then two and a half hours in the afternoon yielded eleven 'keepers.'

Dinner was as fabulous as the night before with bass filets and charcoal-grilled steak. The wine and story-telling was a repeat with the addition of the duet singing a number of songs. The last I heard from my first floor suite was *"Oh Lord it's hard to be humble, when you're perfect in every way. I can't wait to look in the mirror; I get better lookin' each day."*

I'll have to bring my ear plugs again this year.

I was sure I'd be driving on our way home the next day.

The third day started again with yoga overlooking the river. The sky was very different that day. I've never seen it that way. The sunrise in the east cast a light on the river and the west bank leaving the water with a stunning shimmering copper, maybe even a gold color. What a great memory.

9:44 am

Ok, time to quit daydreaming and pay attention to the rest of the day. Let's just go ahead and call Bo so he can arrange the next trip.

Bo's phone rang then went to his answering machine.

"Hey, brother Bo, it's Alex. Your invite to the next Uncle Kent fishing trip is on. Just let me know when. Love ya!"

9:53 am

One hour and ten minutes later Alex was startled by a revelation. She sat up straight in the driver's seat; she nearly drove off the road. She focused, caught her breath and knew she would need to stop at the next exit, or better, the next rest area.

"Dammit!" she yelled out loud. *"I can't believe I didn't think of it before or see it before. Dammit, Dammit."*

Something in her recall and memory jumped out at her.

"It's Uncle Kent. I know it's Uncle Kent. I can't say anything to anybody, including Mom. But I know it's Uncle Kent." He's the one who coordinates all of this. He's the intermediary. I know it's him."

Alex had suddenly realized something about Kent that just jolted body and mind.

"I remember the reeds at his greenhouse when I was there. It was right there, three reeds, empty, herbs and plants all over the yard and gardens. He was assembling the weapons. Dammit!"

Alex stopped at the next rest area and ran around the inside perimeter for ten minutes. She got back in her car, put on her music and continued east. It was both a shock and a relief:

"But, My God, that changes everything."

Alex reminded herself she wouldn't have any contact or have any requests for the next mission for at least thirty days.

The remaining three hours home were with mixed thoughts. She knew she would have to keep this discovery to herself.

At dusk that evening in Cherokee, North Carolina on Qualla Grounds, a small group quietly and secretly celebrated with native American prayers and chants, thanking their Creator for providing Alex with her great strength, wisdom and bravery. Alex's mother learned about what had happened and silently prayed for her daughter as tears filled her eyes and her lips trembled. She could not share this news with anyone.

Alex's Revenge Killing Mindset

An Addendum to

Alex, Cherokee Assassin – Book One

James A. McGregor

Southern Sunsets Publications

Alex's Revenge Killing Mindset

An Addendum to

Alex, Cherokee Assassin – Book One

Copyright © 2017 by James A. McGregor

ISBN: 978-0-9984398-2-2

Southern Sunsets Publications

Georgetown, Florida

"Prior to the Trail of Tears, Cherokee people, men, women and children, were rounded up at gunpoint by United States soldiers and Georgia militia, torn from their homes and forced into removal stockades awaiting removal.

Conditions at the removal fort stockades were reprehensible. Food intended for the tribal people was sold to locals. What little the Cherokee had brought with them was stolen and sold. Living areas were filled with excrement. Cherokee women and children were repeatedly raped. Soldiers forced their captives to perform acts of deprivation so disgusting, abominable and heinous they cannot be told here. One member of the Georgia Guard later wrote, "During the Civil War I watched as hundreds of men died, including my brother, but none of that compares to what we did to the Cherokee Indians." - Excerpt from Alex Cowart term paper Resource: (1) About North Georgia, *Cherokee Removal Forts.*

Alex's mindset and ability to carry out her missions began in her teen years, and was dramatically increased in her late high school and college years through today. It has been led by the horrific death of her father, her studies of the Cherokee history and her outstanding athletic ability and capacity for intense physical exercise that had an outlet in sports and other athletic and outdoor activities. Her curiosity and love of weapons was largely instilled by her brother Bo. Her desire for respect for Cherokee and Indian heritage and history was immense. This came largely from her love and respect of her mother and family.

It was her self-study of Cherokee history as a teenager and the pride as a Cherokee imbedded in her by her immediate family and other relatives that led to her enrollment at University of North

Carolina. Here she was part of a school with a large enrollment of other American Indian students. She met Native American students and faculty with a broad range of mindsets, from peace-loving to militant. Here she could continue her athletic activities. It was here she would learn the true history of the Cherokee Indians – the good, the bad, and the disgusting. Her Senior-year term paper was an accumulation of her college work and Cherokee history studies and her new mindset. It is published below:

"History is the Story of Mankind written by the Victors"

By Alex Cowart, 2003

 The Cherokee Nation is a tragic tale of force wining over decency and power winning over justice. The Eastern Band of Cherokee Indians of Georgia and North Carolina have an amazing story of survival and victory over disgusting evil.

  The history of the Cherokee Nation remains one of the most dramatic, disturbing and shameful acts in the history of the United States Government prompted and promoted by the then Presidents of the United States. It is further dramatic, disturbing and shameful in that it was a co-operative effort between the United States Government and the State of Georgia. The United States had granted the Cherokee nation total sovereignty in 1776 at the time of the formation of the United States as a nation. The two joined forces to defy a Supreme Court Ruling and forcibly remove productive, law-abiding citizens and families of a Sovereign Nation living within their borders, force them into stockades unfit for humans, treat them worse than animals, and forcibly march them for hundreds of miles to rid the State of Georgia of them. It is one of world history's worst cases of ethnic cleansing. It is a story only partially told, written by the victors.

James W. Tyner wrote, in *Those Who Cried, 1993*: *"In the history of world civilizations and nations that have come and gone, there is none that compares with the people of the Cherokee Tribe of Indians. The Cherokees had a civilized Nation, organized and functioning, equal to any other of that time. Their government, economy, social standards, educational system, and religious life were second to none. Yet, the world saw a larger nation devour a smaller nation in the name of hate and greed, the completeness of which the tongue is mute to describe."*Resource: (9) Tyner, James, *Those Who Cried, 1993*.

At the time of Andrew Jackson's Indian Removal Act of 1830 the Cherokee Nation with headquarters in north Georgia was considered by Europeans and European-Americans to be the most civilized tribe in America. Their land, the Cherokee Nation, was granted existence in 1776 as part of the United States of America. They had their own written language, their own newspaper, *The Cherokee Pheonix*, many Cherokee citizens owned large homes and mansions. They owned a wide range of commercial businesses. Like their white counterparts, they owned slaves to work their large tracts of land. They had their own judicial system, their own schools; they built their own roads and bridges. They had significant commercial activities with financial institutions in the United States and England. They traveled to and communicated with representatives of the United States on a nation-to-nation basis, and when they needed to defend their sovereignty they presented two cases regarding their sovereignty to the United States Supreme Court....and won.

Leading up to the 1830s, the arrival of Europeans in the late 1700s and early 1800s and their increasing encroachment on the people and lands of the Cherokee Nation had accelerated the pace of economic and environmental change. By the 1830s, both

Cherokee and whites farmed with plows, reducing precious topsoil. European bounties on predator animals virtually eliminated the wolf, fox, panther and mountain lion. Road building interrupted game paths and caused runoff and silting of streams. Population increases both white and Cherokee, diminished game and nesting sites. Newly introduced plant and animals changed farming preferences, domestic architecture, settlement patterns, landscapes, and trade networks.

The Georgia Cherokees were significant participants in these changes. By the 1830s Cherokees in Georgia owned nearly 80,000 head of livestock. Cotton had been introduced and was becoming a viable crop for Cherokee farmers. Several Cherokees in Georgia – Major Ridge, John Ross, John Martin, Joseph Vann, and James Daniel, for example – were among the wealthiest in the Nation. Property valuations of 1836-1837 enumerated nearly 80,000 fruit trees; 63,000 were peach. Georgia Cherokees of the 1830s owned more than 6,000 dwellings. White and Cherokee co-owned saw mills and grist mills. Further, the 1835 census reveals that Georgia Cherokees cultivated nearly 20,000 acres and produced 269,000 bushels of corn. The following year, they drove 40,000 hogs to middle Alabama and southern Georgia where cotton production had caused food shortages. Resource: (7) New Georgia Encyclopedia, *Cherokee Indians*.

The United States Government and State of Georgia claim that the Indians did not make productive use of their land was wholly inaccurate in the Cherokee lands of Georgia.

White settlers and immigrants had come to Cherokee areas of north Georgia over the 30-plus years prior to the federally mandated removal. For the most part, Cherokees accepted their presence and welcomed the new whites. Intermarriages between white male settlers and Cherokee women were condoned. A large number came as gold miners as a result of the 1828 discovery of gold in Dahlonega area. This coincided with the State of Georgia sponsored, United States Government condoned, land lotteries designed to give land to the new white settlers, facilitate conflicts and remove Cherokees from Georgia. The State of Georgia sold land belonging to the Cherokee nation via their land lotteries without ever taking title or legal possession of the properties. The land was simply stolen from the Cherokees by the State of Georgia. Most oppressive is the fact that this was done five years prior to a treaty between the United States and the Cherokee removing them from Georgia.

In 1830 the Georgia Assembly passed a law abridging the rights of Georgia Cherokees. The seething hatred and greed displayed by the "civilized" European-Americans who held ruling seats in the United States and Georgia Governments had been unleashed. This Georgia legislation specifically prohibited members of the Cherokee Nation the rights to assemble, their rights to free speech, for appearance in court and that they had no rights to the land of the Cherokee Nation. The problem was the citizens of the Cherokee Nation had sovereignty over the State of Georgia. They had been granted a government-to-government relationship with the United States at the time the Cherokee Nation was created.

The unlawful Georgia Act reads as follows:

"ACT OF THE GENERAL ASSEMBLY OF THE State of Georgia. PASSED IN MILLEDGEVILLE AT AN ANNUAL SESSION IN OCTOBER, NOVEMBER AND DECEMBER 1830.

1830 Vol.1 – Pages 114-118

Sequential Number: 088

Full Title: AN ACT to prevent the exercise of assumed and arbitrary power, by all persons under pretext of authority from the Cherokee Indians, and their laws, and to prevent white persons from residing within that part of the chartered limits of Georgia, occupied by the Cherokee Indians, and to provide a guard for the protection of the gold mines, and to enforce the laws of the State within the aforesaid territory.

Be it enacted by the Senate and House of Representatives of the State of Georgia, in General Assembly met, and it is hereby enacted by the authority of the same, That after the first day of February, eighteen hundred and thirty-one, it shall not be lawful for any person, or persons, under colour or pretence, of authority from said Cherokee tribe, or as head men, chiefs, or warriors of said tribe, to cause or procure by any means the assembling of any council, or other Legislative body of the said Indians or others living among them, for the purpose of legislating, (or for any other purpose whatever.) And persons offending against the provisions of this section, shall be guilty of a high misdemeanor, and subject to indictment therefor, and on conviction, shall be punished by confinement at hard labour in the Penitentiary for the space of four years.

Sec.2. And be it further enacted by the authority aforesaid, That after the time aforesaid, it shall not be lawful for any person or persons under pretext of authority from the Cherokee tribe, or as representatives, chiefs, headmen, or warriors of said tribe, to meet, or assemble as a council, assembly, convention, or in any other capacity, for the purpose of making laws, orders, or regulations for said tribe. And all persons offending against the provisions of this section, shall be guilty of a high misdemeanor and subject to an indictment, and on conviction thereof, shall undergo an imprisonment in the Penitentiary at hard labour for

103

the space of four years.

Sec.3. And be it further enacted by the authority aforesaid, That after the time aforesaid, it shall not be lawful for any person or persons, under colour, or by authority, of the Cherokee tribe, or any of its laws or regulations, to hold any court or tribunal whatever, for the purpose of hearing and determining causes either civil or criminal; or to give any judgement in such causes, or to issue, or cause to issue any process against the person or property of any of said tribe. And all persons offending against the provisions of this section, shall be guilty of a high misdemeanor, and subject to indictment, and on conviction thereof, shall be imprisoned in the Penitentiary at hard labor for the space of four years.

Sec.4. And be it further enacted by the authority aforesaid, That after the time aforesaid, it shall not be lawful for any person or persons, as a ministerial officer, or in any other capacity, to execute any precept, command, or process, issued by any court or tribunal in the Cherokee tribe, on the persons or property of any of said tribe. And all persons offending against the provisions of this section, shall be guilty of a trespass and subject to indictment, and on conviction thereof, shall be punished by fine and imprisonment in the jail or in the Penitentiary not longer than four years, at the discretion of the court.

Sec.5. And be it further enacted by the authority aforementioned, That after the time aforesaid, it shall not be lawful for any person, or persons, to confiscate, or attempt to confiscate, or otherwise to cause a forfeiture of the property or estate of any Indian of said tribe, in consequence of his enrolling himself and family for emigration, or offering to enroll for emigration, or any other act of said Indian in furtherance of his intention to emigrate. And persons offending against the provisions of this section, shall be guilty of high misdemeanor, and on conviction, shall undergo an imprisonment in the Penitentiary at hard labor for the space of four years.

Sec.6. And be it further enacted by the authority aforesaid, That none of the provisions of this act, shall be so construed as to prevent said tribe, its headmen, chiefs, or other representatives from meeting with any agent or commissioner, on the part of this State or the United States, for any purpose whatever.

Sec.7. And be it further enacted by the authority aforesaid, That all white persons residing within the limits of the Cherokee nation, on the first day of March next, or at any time thereafter, without a license or permit, from his Excellency the Governor, or from such agent as his Excellency the Governor, shall authorize to grant such permit or license, and who shall not have taken the oath hereinafter required, shall be guilty of an high misdemeanor, and upon conviction thereof, shall be punished by confinement in the Penitentiary at hard labour, for a term not less than four years: *Provided,* that the provisions of this section shall not be so construed, as to extend to any authorized agent or agents, of the government of the United States, or of this State, orto any person or persons, who may rent any of those improvements, which have been abandoned by Indians, who have emigrated West of the Mississippi: *Provided* nothing contained in this section, shall be so construed as to extend to white females, and all male children under twenty-one years of age.

Sec.8. And be it further enacted by the authority aforesaid, That all white persons, citizens of the State of Georgia, who have procured a license in writing, from his Excellency the Governor, or from such agent as his Excellency the Governor, shall authorize to grant such permit or license, to reside within the limits of the Cherokee nation, and who have taken the following oath, viz: - "I,A.B. do solemnly swear (or affirm, as the case may be,) that I will support and defend the Constitution and laws of the State of Georgia, and uprightly demean myself as a citizen thereof, so help me God," shall be, and the same hereby declared, exempt and free from the operation of the seventh section of this act.

Sec.9. And be it further enacted, That his Excellency the Governor, be, and he is hereby authorized to grant licenses to reside within the limits of the Cherokee nation, according to the provisions of the eighth section of this act.

Sec.10. And be it further enacted by the authority aforesaid, That no person shall collect toll from any person for passing any turnpike gate or toll bridge, by authority of any act or law of the Cherokee tribe, or any chief or headman or men, of the same.

Sec.11. And be it further enacted by the authority aforesaid, That his Excellency the Governor, be, and he is hereby empowered, should he deem it necessary, either for the protection of the mines, or for the enforcement of the laws of force within the Cherokee nation, to raise and organize a guard, to be employed on foot or mounted as occasion may require, which shall not consist of more than sixty persons, which guard shall be under the command of the commissioner or agent appointed by the Governor, to protect the mines, with power to dismiss from the service; any member of said guard, on paying the wages due for services rendered, for disorderly conduct, and make appointments to fill the vacancies occasioned by such dismissal.

Sec.12. And be it further enacted by the authority aforesaid, That each person who may belong to said guard; shall receive for his compensation at the rate of fifteen dollars per month when on foot, and at the rate of twenty dollars per month when mounted, for every month that such person is engaged in actual service, and in the event that the commissioner or agent herein referred to, should die, resign or fail to perform the duties herein required of him, his Excellency the Governor, is hereby authorized and required to appoint in his stead, some other fit and proper person to the command of said guard, and the commissioner or agent, having the command of the guard aforesaid, for the better discipline thereof, shall appoint three sergeants who shall receive at the rate of twenty dollars per month, while serving on foot, and twenty-five dollars per month, when mounted, as compensation whilst in actual service.

Sec.13. And be it further enacted by the authority aforesaid, That the said guard , or any member of them, shall be, and they are hereby authorized and empowered to arrest any person legally charged with or detected in, a violation of the laws of this State, and to convey as soon as practicable, the person so arrested before a Justice of the Peace, Judge of the Superior or Justice of Inferior Court, of this State, to be dealt with according to the law, and the pay and support of said guard be provided out of the fund, already appropriated for the protection of the gold mines.

/s/ ASBURY HULL,

Speaker of the House of Representatives.

/s/ THOMAS STOCKS,

107

President of the Senate.

/s/ GEORGE R. GILMER, Governor"

With the wind of victory at its back, the Georgia legislators had seen their opportunity to finally eliminate Cherokees from their land and cover their tracks for the illegally seized land sold in the land lotteries. In 1831 Georgia distributed 18,500 parcels of land of the Cherokee Nation following the States' illegal seizure of the land. Andrew Jackson had become President of the United States in March 1829 and was certain to pass and implement the Indian Removal Act of 1830.

In 1831 Georgia militia arrested Samuel Worcester for residing on Cherokee lands without a state permit, imprisoning him in Milledgeville, Georgia. In *Worcester v. Georgia (1832)*, the U.S. Supreme Court Chief Justice John Marshall ruled that American Indian nations were "distinct, independent political communities retaining their original natural rights," and entitled to federal protection from the actions of state governments that infringe on their sovereignty. President Andrew Jackson ignored the supreme courts' ruling stating, "John Marshall has made his decision, let him enforce it now if he can." Jackson's landslide reelection in 1832 had emboldened calls for Cherokee removal by Jackson and Georgia's government leaders. His rationale for his belief and the pursuit of the Indian Removal policy was stated that it was an effort to prevent the Cherokee from facing extinction as a people. This misguided belief was wrong for two reasons: First, Several thousand Cherokee had already moved to Arkansas and Oklahoma between 1817 and 1832 and were settled there at the threats from Georgia and the United States governments and militia. These "early settlers" were supposedly safe from annihilation from the U.S. government. Second, the area of the

Cherokee nation was in a state of economic surplus and could have continued to accommodate both the Cherokee and the new white settlers. It was plainly a matter of greed, racism and hatred. It was the same mindset that was adopted by and drove Adolf Hitler to the mass murder of German and Polish Jews 100 years later.

Though it is not commonly known, western migration of the Citizens of the Cherokee nation began well before the final removal and Trail of Tears in 1838. By that time approximately one-third of the Cherokee Nation people were already residing in Oklahoma. With mounting pressure, the United States entered treaties with the Cherokee in 1817 and 1818 for the purpose of acquiring land in the east. Out of these treaties the Cherokee citizens had a choice of two alternatives. They could either enroll to move to the west or they could file for a reservation of 640 acres in the Cherokee Nation – which would revert to the state of Georgia upon their death or abandonment. [Such a deal! Give them some of their own land with a guarantee that they would give it back to the state.] Only 622 Cherokee citizens applied. Of those who did apply and pledge to stay, very few of the 622 were chosen to receive land. Resource (2) Blankenship, Bob, *Cherokee Roots, Volume I, 1992.*

Stated again, in the late 1820s and early 1830s, the State of Georgia simply claimed all the land of the Cherokee Nation and sold it to white settlers via land lotteries.

From 1830 on, Cherokee Nation citizens continued to be harassed and confronted with their futures by the United States and Georgia militia. Illegal removal forts or stockades or holding pens were built on Cherokee Nation lands by the United States intended to house the remaining Cherokee people long before their journey on the Trail of Tears. Sources list 15 forts on Cherokee Nation lands including one at New Echota, the Capital of the Cherokee Nation.

Earliest of the removal forts in Georgia was Camp Hiler Sixes in what is now Cherokee County, Georgia, was built in September 1830 shortly after the United States Congress passed the Indian Removal Act. This camp was used to house members of the infamous Georgia Guard who took it upon themselves to brutalize the Cherokee after the *Cherokee Nation v. Georgia, 1831* Supreme Court ruling in which the Supreme Court refused to hear the case about Georgia's extending its laws on the Cherokee thereby agreeing with the Cherokee. The construction of the remaining removal forts sped up. Resource: (1) About North Georgia, *Cherokee Removal Forts.*

With great concern, Cherokee Principal Chief John Ross along with several other Cherokee leaders journeyed to Washington to meet with President Andrew Jackson. Jackson hypocritically told them "You shall remain in your ancient land as long as grass grows and water runs."Jackson simply lied. Resource: (1) About North Georgia, *Cherokee Removal Forts.*

In the meantime the state of Georgia had already illegally taken the land of the Cherokee Nation and sold it by land lotteries. Andrew Jackson and the United States Government stood by and watched. With the continuing harassment and fear of extermination by the Georgia and United States militia, the leaders moved the Capital of the Cherokee Nation from New Echotato Red Clay, Tennessee, just north of the Georgia border.

From 1832 to 1835 life for the Cherokee people in the Cherokee Nation was hopeful but uneasy. Work on the removal forts and work on improving roads for the removal continued. In December

1835, a U.S. Treaty Commissioner summoned the entire Cherokee Nation to New Echota, the former Capital of the Cherokee Nation. His warning to them was that all who failed to attend would be regarded as approving the actions taken there. Only a few hundred Cherokee attended out of the 17,000 tribal members. Major Ridge led the Cherokee attendees; however, they were not authorized to sign on behalf of the Cherokee Nation. They illegally approved a treaty that had previously been rejected twice, that all Cherokee people move west by 1838. This treaty, the Treaty of New Echota, gave President Jackson the excuse and power to move ahead with the removal in spite of his knowledge that the leaders of the Cherokee Nation had not signed the treaty and had not attended the meeting in New Echota and that 15,000 Cherokee people had signed a petition against signing the treaty. The United States Senate approved the treaty by one vote.

In 1836 and 1837 small groups of Cherokee Nation citizens left for the new land west of the Mississippi and joined those who had moved years earlier. Others moved to remote areas of North Carolina, Tennessee and north Georgia. The May 1838 removal deadline was near. Nearly 17,000 Cherokee clung to their hopes and homelands. President van Buren, Jackson's successor, dispatched 7,000 military and militia into the lands of the Cherokee Nation to impound the Cherokee people in the removal fort stockades.

Removal operations began on May 18, 1838, mostly carried out by the Georgia Guard. The first Cherokee round-up under orders from United States General Winfield Scott started on May 25th. The round-up lasted 26 days. Squads of military and militia scoured the area. Cherokee men were seized from behind their plows; women were dragged from their homes. Entire families were plucked from their homes, often separated. Most of the

Cherokees who were herded to the stockades had only time to take the clothes they were wearing. Their homes, furnishings, valuables and other personal belongings along with their farms and livestock fell prey to whites who followed the removal round-up squads. They were reported as looting homes and graves stripping the corpses of silver pendants and valuables. A Georgia volunteer who later served as a Colonel in the Confederate Army said years afterwards, "I fought through the Civil War and have seen many men shot to pieces and slaughtered by the thousands, the Cherokee removal was the cruelest work I ever knew." Resource: (6) Hudson, Charles, *The Southeastern Indians,* University of Tennessee Press, 1999.

Conditions at the removal fort stockades were reprehensible. Food intended for the tribal members was sold to locals. What little the Cherokee had brought with them was stolen and sold. Living areas were filled with excrement. Birth rates among the Cherokee dropped to near zero during the months of captivity. Cherokee women and children were repeatedly raped. Soldiers forced their captives to perform acts of deprivation so disgusting, abominable and heinous they cannot be told here. One member of the Georgia Guard later wrote, "During the Civil War I watched as hundreds of men died, including my brother, but none of that compares to what we did to the Cherokee Indians."Resource: (1) About North Georgia, *Cherokee Removal Forts.*

Yes, the story and written history of the Cherokee Indians has been filtered by the victors. Andrew Jackson is still revered as a great military leader and President of the United States. We see his face daily on the U.S. twenty-dollar bill. Yet he is America's Adolph Hitler.   And, yes, history should record the State of Georgia as the most racist state in the history of the United States.

April 12, 2003

Resources:

(1) About North Georgia, *Cherokee Removal Forts.*
(2) Blankenship, Bob, *Cherokee Roots, Volume I, 1992.*
(3) Ehle, John, *Trail of Tears, The Rise and Fall of the Cherokee Nation,* Anchor Publishing, 1997.
(4) Finger, John R., *The Eastern Band of Cherokee 1819 – 1900,* 1984.
(5) Garrison, Tim Allen, *The Legal Ideology of Removal, The Southern Judiciary and the Sovereignty of Native American Nations,* 2002.
(6) Hudson, Charles, *The Southeastern Indians,* University of Tennessee Press, 1999.
(7) New Georgia Encyclopedia, *Cherokee Indians.*
(8) Time-Life Books; *Tribes of the Southern Woodlands,* The American Indian Series.
(9) Tyner, James W., *Those Who Cried, 1993,* Unknown Binding."

According to author Napoleon Hill, "Through some strange and powerful principal of 'mental chemistry' which she has never divulged, [Mother] Nature wraps up in the impulse of strong desire, 'that something' which recognizes no such word as impossible and accepts no such reality as failure." And further, "Because we have the power to control our thoughts, our brain becomes magnetized with the dominant thoughts we hold in our minds. These 'magnets' attract the forces, the people, the circumstances of life which harmonize with our dominating thoughts." Thus, we succeed in our cause.

Alex's new mindset had been established. Appropriate revenge could now be an integral part of her life.

At age twenty-one, Alex was referred by a family friend to

consider participating in a new program focusing on Native Americans combating local and regional terrorism. The program included the acceptance of revenge killing. An appropriate outlet for her mindset was discovered. Her agreement to participate in the program would change her life forever.

About the Author

James A. McGregor is a Florida-based writer with numerous years of experience working with and writing about North American Indians. His works include historical writings, petitions for tribal federal recognition, blog posts and fiction. He also writes and publishes articles regarding casinos and racetrack/casinos in the southeastern United States. McGregor's current works include the Alex- Cherokee Assassin series, and his blog posts on www.casinotesracinotes.com.